A life which does not go into action is a failure.
—Arnold J. Toynbee, *A Study of History*

Okay, maybe they're correct and I don't know right from wrong, but this much I do know—it isn't enough to simply *believe* in something. To be truly alive, you have to be ready to *die* for something. Harder still, there are times when you have to be willing to *kill* for something. I am both ready to die and willing to kill.
—Mack Bolan, THE EXECUTIONER

THE EXECUTIONER:
Continental Contract

by

Don Pendleton

PINNACLE BOOKS • NEW YORK CITY

THE EXECUTIONER: CONTINENTAL CONTRACT

An original Pinnacle Books edition, published for the first time anywhere.

ISBN: 0-523-00405-2

First printing, January, 1971
Second printing, April, 1971
Third printing, September, 1971
Fourth printing, November, 1971
Fifth printing, December, 1971
Sixth printing, June, 1972
Seventh printing, July, 1972
Eighth printing, November, 1972
Ninth printing, March, 1974
Tenth printing, March, 1975
Eleventh printing, September, 1975

Printed in the United States of America

PINNACLE BOOKS, INC.
275 Madison Avenue
New York, N.Y. 10016

Prologue

Mack Bolan's war with the Mafia was only a few months old, and already the man had become a legend and a modern day folk hero. Law enforcement agencies at every level of government and throughout the land had taken to keeping a special file on the exploits of the man known as *The Executioner*, and various foreign capitals would soon be added to the alert network of international police organizations. Others, also, sought the lifeblood of Mack Bolan. It was common knowledge that a $100,000 death contract had been issued against Bolan by the ruling council of bosses of that vast "invisible second government" known as the Mafia, or *La Cosa Nostra.* This was an "open contract," with bounty hunters of every walk and stripe invited and encouraged to participate in the hunt. It was also being rumored that various individual family bosses had added attractive bonuses to the final payoff in the event that the murder contract was closed in their territory; it has been estimated that in several areas of the country, Bolan's head would be worth a quarter of a million dollars to his killer.

What sort of superman could inspire such nationwide awe, fear, and respect from both sides of a modern society? Bolan himself would be the last man to attempt to answer that question. He knew that he was no superman. Like any other man, he bled when wounded, trembled when frightened, felt loneliness in isolation, and regarded life as preferable to death.

Short months earlier, this "superman" had been on combat duty in Vietnam, in his own eyes just another non-com fighting another version of the impossible war. But in that war had been comrades, a sense of national purpose, and the brawn and brains of the United States government backing him. Now he was alone, often doubting his own moral imperatives, and with only his own abilities and instincts to stand against what often seemed to be the entire world.

When Bolan killed enemies in Vietnam, he was decorated for heroism and applauded by the bulk of his society. When he killed the enemy at home, he was charged with murder and hounded as a dangerous threat to that same society. In that other war had been respites from combat, a reasonably safe place to lay the head and rest the soul; in this new war were no places to pause, no zones of safety, no sanctuaries for the man whose battlefield was the entire world and whose enemies were both infinite and often invisible.

No—Mack Bolan was no superman, and none knew this better than himself.

Bolan was perhaps a bit too modest in his assessments of self, however. He had received the tag "The Executioner" by virtue of his unusual military specialty in Vietnam. A sniper team sharpshooter, the young sergeant had repeatedly penetrated hostile territories and strongholds, often spending many days behind enemy lines on deep-penetration strikes against Viet Cong terrorist leaders and officials. Steely nerves, precision tactics, and remarkable self-sufficiency had spelled the difference for sniper Bolan, the difference which had kept him alive and functioning through two full combat tours in Southeast Asia and earned him the respect and admiration of superiors and peers alike. But Sgt. Bolan had been much more than a sniper. Executing an important defector or enemy field commander on his own soil could be a ticklish business. Merely locating and identifying the target in unfamiliar territory was challenge enough; to then make the strike, hang around long enough to verify the success of the mission, and then to safely withdraw through miles of aroused hostile country required considerable personal resources.

Bolan had obviously possessed those resources. He had been regarded as a highly valuable weapon of the psychological warfare being waged for the soul of Vietnam. Now it appeared that Bolan, along with legions of other young Americans, had lost his own soul in that conflict—a point which many homefront moralizers were hastening to make. He had been editorialized as "a government-trained mad dog," and lamented on the floor of the U.S. Senate as "America's military sins coming home to roost."

All this was inconsequential to Mack Bolan. He had not expected medals for his war at home. He would admit, even, that his initial strike against the Mafia had been largely motivated by a desire for vengeance. His parents and teen-aged sister had died violently as a result of Mafia terrorism and the police had seemed helpless to do anything about it. Bolan had not been helpless, and he had done something about it. He took his pound of flesh from the Sergio Frenchi family and his sense of personal justice was satisfied in the lightning strikes that left that Mafia arm in shambles. Long before that first battle had ended, however, Mack Bolan came to realize that he had entered into another war without end. The mob would not, *could* not hold still for that sort of treatment. The entire premise for their survival was based on the idea of their invincibility and omnipresence in the American society. They had to crush Bolan and run his head up their pole for all to see and beware.

Bolan's war thus became a holy war, good versus evil, and he clung to this battle philosophy as his only buttress against a disapproving society. And as the war waged on, from front to successive front, his growing familiarity with the syndicate served to intensify this certain feeling that he was fighting the most vicious enemy to ever threaten his nation. The mob was everywhere, in everything—controlling, manipulating, corrupting, wielding an influence such as no political party had ever dared dream. Invisibly they reached out to touch every man, woman, and child in the country—stealing more from the poor than from the rich—squeezing the working man with invisible taxes and tributes, demoralizing and enslaving the young with drugs and insidiously corruptive pleasures, cannibalizing industry and victimizing both retailers and consumers, seizing the reins of government through blackmail and the exploitation of human greed—and everything they touched turned rotten and spoiled and ugly and corrupt. This was Mack Bolan's vision, and his sustaining truth, and his reason for living when often the most pleasurable thing possible would be to merely die.

He earned distinction as *The Executioner* in the jungles and hamlets of Vietnam and it was this same brand of warfare that he brought to the American continent. A police lieutenant in Pittsfield, Bolan's home town and scene of his first Mafia encounter, was responsible for the nickname living on through the transition from Vietnam to hometown—but it was Bolan alone who endowed the name with the terrible attributes that rocked the Mafia ship of state and struck dread deep into the bones of *Mafiosi* everywhere, from the lowest street soldier to the most exalted *Capo.*

The Executioner was not a cop; he could go and do as no cop could. The Executioner was not a judge or jury; he was not interested in legal technicalities, bribes, or threats. The Executioner was not a prison guard or trusty; he was not impressed with political or underworld influence and intimidation, and he had no reasons whatever for granting special favors or dispensations. He was incorruptible, non-negotiable, ready to die, and willing to kill; he was *THE EXECUTIONER,* and his target was the Mafia, *La Cosa Nostra,* anywhere and everywhere, so long as he should live.

1: The Dulles Trap

For one frozen heartbeat, Mack Bolan knew that he was a dead man. And then the moment ticked on, recording the confusion and hesitation and perhaps even awe in the eyes of the adversary, and Bolan lived on. Trained instincts of the jungle fighter responded one flashing synapse quicker; Bolan's reaction to the surprise encounter was a total one as mind and body exploded into the challenge for survival. His left chopped against the gun even as the yawning bore of the .45 thundered its greetings, his knee lifting high in the same reflex as he twisted into the attack. The shot went wild, the gun clattered to the ground, and the foe momentarily rode Bolan's knee, buckaroo style, then he was groaning groundward and rolling into a spasmodic knot.

Bolan scooped up the .45 in a continuation of the defensive reflex and was swinging into the lineup on the fallen opponent when his corner-vision warned him of activity on the flank. He whirled and rapidfired three rounds in the general direction of that threat. Answering fire immediately triangulated on him as shadowy shapes rapidly dispersed and went to ground some twenty yards distant. A thick voice yelled, "It's him awright—now waitaminnit, Bolan!"

Bolan was not waiting. He stepped around the writhing Mafioso and jogged quietly to the far corner of the building. A gun boomed from that quarter and a slug punched into the wall beside him. He jerked back and returned warily to his former position where he stared down at the suffering man, grimly assessing his possibilities of escape and quietly damning himself for walking into the setup.

The same thick voice from the darkness called out, "Wise up, Bolan. You're sewed in. Throw out the gun, then put your hands where we can see 'em and come talk to us."

Bolan knew how that conversation would go—with a six-figure bounty on his head. He also knew that this gun crew was not at Dulles International Airport to convoy a nickel-and-dime air freight hijack operation; Executioner Bolan had been suckered. What had begun as a soft surveillance of Mafia activity had quickly escalated into a full firefight, and Bolan could read nothing into the unhappy development except *ambush.* He gave them credit; they had played it cool. And now he was wondering just how long they had been onto his interest in the airfreight operation. Knowing this, he would know also how elaborately planned was the ambush. If it had been a hasty, last-minute set, then perhaps he stood a chance of busting out. But if they had come there in force, expecting Bolan to walk in . . .

He knelt and placed the muzzle of the .45 against the fallen Mafioso's temple. "How many are out there?" he inquired quietly. "What's the set?"

The man was in a paralysis of torment, and obviously cared little whether he lived or died. He made a faint attempt to respond, partially uncurled himself, then quickly drew back into the knot and vomited. Bolan grimaced with sympathy and stood up, leaning against the building and breathing as softly as possible, ears straining to tell him what his eyes could not.

Frozen time moved sluggishly as he assessed the situation. He could hear them moving about out there in the darkness, closing, consolidating the jaws of the trap. A big jet was taking off from the far side of the airport, another was landing close by, its landing lights probing the darkness as it swept low past the warehouse area—though not close enough to affect Bolan's situation. He was in a section of the sprawling complex which normally saw little or no activity at this hour of the night, a pre-customs storage area. Perhaps even the gunplay had gone unnoticed in the other noises of the huge air terminal.

"What about it, Bolan?" asked the voice out there.

He snapped his .32 out of the sideleather and quickly inspected the load, then threw the appropriated .45 into the open. It clattered loudly as it slid along the concrete ramp, adding another grotesque note to the sounds about him.

Some one called out, "Watch it! He's probably got Joe's gun too!"

Bolan snapped a round toward the voice and was rewarded with a muffled yelp and a returning volley of fire. Meanwhile he had spun off as he fired, crouching and running along the shadows of the warehouse, his eyes alert to the sudden eruption of muzzle flashes. The fusillade tore into the area he had just vacated, and a gasping groan behind him told of the effect upon the writhing Mafioso who had been identified as "Joe."

A voice crowed, "He's hit!"

"Watch it, he's tricky!"

"Not *that* tricky."

"Well, you just waitaminnit, dammit."

Bolan had located the enemy forces, as revealed by the last volley. They were clumped into four groups of about three men each. Two groups were directly across from him, in the shadows of the opposite building; the other two were flanking him, covering from the warehouses to either side of Bolan's position. The leader was out front, as evidenced by the voice of authority; a sub-*regime* was off to the left flank, the cocky voice of impatience and disrespect for the Executioner's image.

The groups out front would have to cross a wide area of relative light in order to close on Bolan. Either flank, however, could move in with only a momentary exposure between the buildings. The tactical instincts of the professional soldier had instantly become aware of this truth, and Bolan was ready to exploit this single favorable factor.

"Bolan?" came the voice from out front.

The wounded *Mafioso* groaned again, feeble and pained, a convincing sound of approaching death. Bolan tensed and waited.

"I told you he's hit!" This from the left flank.

"Dammit you hold it!" From the center. "How you know that ain't Joe?"

"Aw shit, you know better! Joe didn't live a second, face to face with that guy! We can't wait around all night. Cops are gonna be . . ."

Bolan was satisfied that the time had come. He was rolling slowly toward the edge of the shadow, silently putting as much distance as he dared between himself and the building and straining toward a midpoint position toward the left flank. They would be coming in any second now.

"Awright, check 'im out," came the grudging instructions from up front, verifying Bolan's prediction. "Bolan—if you're listening—you fire once, just once, and you're gonna get blasted to hamburger."

The prospective hamburger was lying prone with pistol extended toward the shaft of moonlight falling across his left flank. Cautiously moving feet scraped the concrete out there as a crouching figure leapt across the lighted zone. Bolan held his breath and his fire; another man hurtled over, and then another. The Executioner smiled grimly to himself over that fatal mistake; the entire left flank had moved in, leaving none to protect their own rear. He heard them moving cautiously into the trap as he moved also in a silent circling, and then they were between him and the building and he was sighting down from his prone position, rolling swiftly now and squeezing off a single shot for a calculated effect.

A grunted exclamation of alarm and a confused volley from his original position signalled the success of step two of the bold escape plan; reflexive fire came in from the front and the other flank and the trap closed fully with the *Mafiosi* firing into each other's positions in a contagion of over-reaction.

Bolan himself was on his feet and sprinting into the open flank, leaping across the thin shaft of moonlit area and disappearing into the shadows beyond.

An excited voice cried, "Hold it, we're shooting at each other! Th' bastard's behind us!"

Indeed, the Executioner was behind them. He could hear them shouting and damning one another for their fatal error, the groans and frightened cries of the wounded becoming a cacaphony which was now entirely too familiar and increasingly repugnant to Mack

Bolan. But this was the world he had built for himself, Bolan kept remembering; it was the only one available to him now.

He reached the small van truck which only moments before had been receiving looted pharmaceutical supplies from a darkened warehouse, the object of Bolan's earlier surveillance and once hopefully the lever into the Family's Washington area operations. The lever had become a boomerang, and now Bolan had more of a bite into the Family than he'd anticipated.

The cab door of the truck stood open and the driver was gaping at him across the hood; two men who had been loading the van stood indecisively just inside the warehouse, uncertainly poised between fight and flight. With the ominous appearance of Bolan's .32, they opted for flight and moved hastily into the interior of the building. Bolan waved the pistol in a tight circle encompassing the driver and said, "You too, beat it."

Wordlessly, the driver went into the warehouse and closed the door behind him. Bolan swung in behind the steering wheel of the truck, meshed the gears, and spun about in a rapid acceleration just as the regrouped remnants of the gun crew pounded into the vehicle lane and again opened fire. He dropped low in the seat and swerved into their midst, scattering them and momentarily disrupting their attack, then he was grinding past and careening into a power turn at the corner of the warehouse and the van was taking hits like puncturing hail. He felt a wheel tremor, then vibrate into a wallowing rumble. The clumsy vehicle lunged out of control, scraped the side of the building, rebounded, and plowed into a raised loading ramp an instant after Bolan had leapt clear. The truck partially climbed the ramp then overturned and fell to its side in a screech of grinding metal.

Bolan's own vehicle was parked just beyond the next warehouse, spotted into an escape corridor, and this was his goal. He was running along in the shadows as the Mafia gun crew carefully explored the wreckage of the van, and as he cleared the corner he heard an excited command: "He's not here! Spread out! Al, you take the north side; Benny, the south. Rest o' you guys . . ."

Bolan was in his MG and cranking away in a full power run when a fast moving figure darted out of a shadow and began futilely pumping away at him with a handgun. At the far end of the building another began unloading on him. He took no hits and was settling down with a sigh of relief as he hurtled into the Y leading from the freight area, then he noted the flare of headlamps as two vehicles swung onto the road to his right. Bolan took the left leg, powering into the turn that would take him toward the main air terminal. His first suspicion had proven correct; he had blundered into a massive mantrap, the end of which he had not yet seen. Another pair of vehicles were swinging in above him; there would be at least one more gauntlet to run.

Bolan was weary, and his belly was just about full of open warfare. For a split second he debated ending it here and now. It would be simple and relatively painless—a quiet matter of stopping the MG at the barricade ahead, the final shootout, then blissful oblivion. Already, however, he was there, the trap cars were seesawed across the narrow roadway, and Bolan's intellectual centers stood aside for survivalist instincts. He was powering into the barricade at full throttle. Men with startled faces were flinging themselves clear of the certain collision, and Bolan's hands and feet were quivering with the tension born of a necessity for hair-breadth control and precision timing. He hit brakes and steering and powershift simultaneously, arcing into a half-spin and ricocheting off the barricade into a shallow ditch at the side of the road, jouncing against the chainlink fencing enclosing the runway area—the wheels spinning, finding traction, then propelling him into a surging advance along the sloping walls of the ditch. An alarmed face was giving him the death look from just beyond the MG's hood as human reactions fell one pace behind charging machinery; he heard the whump and saw the body spinning away; a flailing hand thwacked against his door post; then he was climbing for asphalt and making it and the high-traction drive was finding hard surface once more and the scene was falling behind. Only then did the impotent and receding rattle of gunfire officially mark the roadblock a failure; it seemed that Bolan was home clean—the trap had developed lockjaw. His heart had just begun beating again when he saw the police beacons flashing along the perimeter highway. Of course—it was time for the cops to crash the party, and they were coming in force. Bolan counted six cruisers in a tailgate parade, and he knew that there would be no exit from Dulles International this night.

It was a time for decision. The Executioner had never challenged police authority; he had, in fact, studiously avoided any confrontation that would force him into a gunfight with cops. It seemed now, however, that the unavoidable moment had arrived. First they would seal all exits, then they would pour the place full of bluesuits, the inexorable magic of police methodology would have its way, and that final inevitable staredown with authority would occur. Bolan would not submit to arrest, he knew that. Better to die swiftly and with the dignity of a still-free man than to suffer that slow suffocation of jail cells and courtrooms. How strong, though, were his instincts for survival? In that final moment when he was staging his apeshit charge and inviting them to cut him down, would those combat reflexes assert themselves as they had so many times before, would his fire be going in for effect, and would he end up taking one or two good men with him? This was one of Bolan's most persistent nightmares; he had met a cop or two during the course of his Mafia war, had recognized them as soldiers doing a soldier's job and respected them for it. He did not wish to kill or maim any cops.

So now the mob was at his rear and the bluesuits were pushing in from the front. Bolan made a swift decision and pulled into the parking area of the passenger terminal. He took a briefcase and a small suitcase from the rear of the MG and left the battered vehicle snuggled into the sea of cars in a longterm parking space. As he reached the terminal, two police cruisers were flashing along the inner drive; from the other direction, a small caravan of private autos were hurrying up from the freight area.

Bolan sighed and went on in. He was caught in the pincers. Possibly, one escape route remained open. Straight up. It was fly or die—and, for Mack Bolan, the war-weary one man army, that initial decision was merely to fly now, die later, for he knew that death awaited him between every heartbeat.

This was to be a fateful decision for certain overseas arms of that cancerous crime syndicate known as the Mafia. Though he did not know it at that moment, Mack Bolan's private war was about to become an international one. The Executioner was moving toward a new front.

2: *Movements at the Front*

The tall man, lean and rangy in a dark suit and coordinated pastel shirt and tie, strode into the deserted flightline waiting room and dropped a small overnight bag and a briefcase carelessly to the floor. A shock of black hair spilled across the forehead, large tinted lenses in gold wire frames concealed the eyes, a heavy moustache trailed out to almost meet sideburns at the jawline. Just outside, the ramp dispatcher was standing in front of a big jet and passing hand signals to the cockpit crew; the engines of the huge airliner were whining into the warmup run.

The uniformed man at the ticket desk widened his eyes noticeably when the hundred dollar bill came into view. The tall man with the eyeshades told him, "I'll bet a hundred you can't get me on that Paris flight."

The ticket man grinned at Bolan and replied, "I'll take that bet, sir." He nudged the man beside him and commanded, "Run out there and tell Andy to hold the gangway, we have a late boarding VIP."

Moments later Bolan was ticketed and moving along the boarding ramp. A man in airline uniform stood impatiently at the aircraft door. He waved the tardy boarder inside and closed the door behind him. Bolan found his seat and was buckling himself in when the door again opened and another last-minute fare stepped inside and took the final remaining open seat, just across the aisle from Bolan. Immediately thereafter the aircraft began moving away from the loading zone.

Bolan was discreetly studying the man across the aisle; what he saw gave him neither comfort nor qualms. He was just a guy, about Bolan's age and size, modishly dressed, still breathing hard from his dash to the plane. A stewardess detached herself from the group at the crew station and came down to add their names to the passenger list. Bolan gave the name on his passport, Stefan Ruggi, and heard the other man identify himself as Gil Martin. This produced a sharp reaction from the stewardess, prompting the man to hastily add, "Look, don't make a fuss, eh? I'll keep the secret if you will."

The girl nodded mute acquiesence and moved forward toward the flight deck. Bolan wondered who the hell was Gil Martin, but his attention was immediately diverted to the window. The plane was moving slowly along a taxiway, running parallel to the terminal building. Considerable activity beyond the fence had commanded Bolan's attention as he noted cars with flashing beacons on their roofs and uniformed men moving energetically about the terminal area. He sighed inwardly and tried to relax into the seat, but the rather plain young woman seated next to him softly exclaimed, "Oh God!"

"Is something wrong?" Bolan inquired, turning to inspect her for the first time.

"Did you see all that out there?"

Bolan smiled. "The police? Are you on the lam?"

The question both amused and embarassed her. "No," she replied, "but doesn't it give you a little tingle to wonder what they're doing? Maybe there's a bomb aboard this plane . . . or a hijacker."

Bolan tried to reassure her. "More than likely it's only super security for a visiting dignitary."

The woman said, "Oh," but was obviously not wholly satisfied with such an un-tingling explanation.

Bolan dismissed her from his mind and tried to force the tensions out also. They would not go. He would not be breathing easy, he knew, until he was off and clear of that aircraft. If the police were as thorough as he knew they could be, a surprise party might be awaiting his arrival in Paris—or, as bad, a Mafia reception—those guys could be thorough, too.

A domestic flight would have been greatly preferable. But this had been the only flight immediately leaving Dulles and it had seemed his best move. Now he was having doubts. He would have to clear through the French customs and perhaps go through other formalities. The only problem with that, in Bolan's view, was his passport. How good was it? He had barely glanced at it, as part of the portfolio urged upon him by Harold Brognola in Miami; he had never seriously entertained any ideas of leaving the country. Could that passport be gimmicked as some weird sort of trap to identify the Executioner the moment he stepped onto foreign soil? No—that would not make sense. Bolan did not wish to go off the deep end of groundless fears—he had enough of the flesh-and-blood variety to occupy his attention.

He glanced at the woman seated next to him and tried to draw a mental equivalent of her fears and his. Wasn't he being just as silly? Was this Mafia war finally getting to his inner chambers, rattling them, raising phantasms of fear much more terrible than the physical reality?

Was Bolan the Bold going to cop out to combat fatigue?

He was thusly talking himself out of an impulse to drag the briefcase into his lap and inspect that passport. They were standing just off the runway now, and the engines were revving up. The door to the flight cabin opened and the stewardess for Bolan's section reappeared. A man in uniform showed himself momentarily in the open doorway, glanced at the passenger identified as Gil Martin and smiled, then closed the door. The stewardess was buckling herself into a seat. She, too, turned and sent a smile toward Martin. If the subject of the curious interest took notice, he did not respond.

Bolan again fell to wondering about the man, then he subconsciously resolved the passport conflict by suddenly opening his briefcase and transferring the passport to the breast pocket of his coat, where it belonged anyway.

Then they were on the takeoff run. Dulles was becoming a blur beyond the window, the nose lifted, and Bolan was being gently pressed into the seat cushions.

For a few hours, okay, he could relax now. The police had allowed the plane to depart. Bolan wondered how much he owed that to the last-minute arrival of Gil Martin, an obvious celebrity who would fit rather well the general Bolan description. He could visualize the exchange between tower and pilot: the police were looking for a tall man, about thirty, dark, clean-shaven, a hard looking bastard with cold brown eyes. He might have boarded the Paris flight at the last moment. Yes, we got a guy like that but, ha ha, it's just old Gil Martin, you know, the celebrity.

The tensions were leaving. Bolan was grateful for the false facial hair which so altered his appearance; doubly grateful that young men's fashions had gone to hair—there was nothing unusual or even notable about face hair these days. The muttonchop sideburns and sweeping moustache gave Bolan an almost soft anonymity. So okay, relax now and conserve the energy, replenish the brain, cool down the vital juices, take it easy. In Paris, he would very likely need everything he could get going, false hair notwithstanding.

Out of his fog of introspection he became aware again of the girl beside him. She was talking compulsively to the passenger in the window seat, apparently fighting takeoff anxieties. ". . . and they say the Right Bank has become so commercial, so brassy, I'd love to find a little hotel on the Left Bank, perhaps in the Sorbonne district. Don't you think that would be charming? And inexpensive, too. They say it's so colorful and interesting, the artists and students and all live there, on the Left Bank I mean, but then on second thought I don't know, I mean it might not be safe for . . ."

Bolan grinned, closed his eyes, and let it all go. He would take care of Paris when Paris presented itself. But only for a little while. A war at home awaited him, commanded him. Maybe he could work in a brief R&R in gay Paree before returning to the front.

The Executioner would soon discover, however, that the entire world was his front. There was to be no R&R for Mack Bolan in gay Paree.

Quick Tony Lavagni sat at a desk in the rear of a shop in Washington's ghetto, counting the day's bag from the most lucrative numbers operation south of Harlem. Wilson Brown, an immense black man and Lavagni's central controller, stood nonchalantly at

Quick Tony's elbow, chewing on a dead cigar and watching the count with miss-nothing eyes. Brown was in his early thirties, and the mark of many personal wars, mostly lost ones, was ground into his dusky features; only the eyes showed an aliveness, a quick awareness and responsiveness, perhaps an intelligent wariness mixed with an acceptance of a black man's destiny. Lavagni was in his forties, not appreciably lighter in color than his controller, an emotional man of quick temper, violent tendencies, and a reputation with a knife. It was this latter consideration that had given him the label of "Quick Tony."

Near the front door lolled two of Brown's runners, talking in bored whispers and shooting occasional dark looks toward the men at the desk. Another white man sat in a chair tilted against the wall, trying to read a racing form in the dim light reaching him from the desk lamp.

Lavagni completed the count, consulted the bank sheet, and drawled, "You're fifty short, Wils."

"Naw," the black man replied, bending low over Lavagni's shoulder to peer at the figures. "It's there in th' side money."

"Oh yeah, I see. You laid off to Georgetown. How come so much lay off, Wils?"

"I told you, we could get flattened if—" Brown's explanation was interrupted by a muted ringing of the telephone. He scooped it up and grunted into the mouthpiece, chewed the cigar furiously for a moment as he listened to the message, then said, "Okay, then you better try to spread another fifty across the worst numbers. You know what, okay?"

"Another *fifty?*" Lavagni fumed as the black man hung up the phone.

"You'll be glad tomorrow," Brown assured him. "It's just one of those days, Tony. It's heavy on all the possibles. We're even having trouble placing lay-offs."

The Italian growled something unintelligible and began placing the money in a heavy paper bag.

Brown raised his eyebrows in surprise. "You takin' the whole bank, Tony?"

"Damn right," Lavagni growled. "You send a boy over tomorrow with a voucher, I'll give 'im the pay-off purse."

"Suddenly Wils Brown ain't to be trusted?" the big man asked in a thickening voice.

"Hey, don't start that—you know me better than to start that, Wils. It's this Bolan. He's been spotted around town, I told you that. I ain't taking no chances on him busting up my banks."

"I thought you were skinnin' that cat, man."

"Yeah, well, certain people are taking care of that detail right now. So don't—" Lavagni was interrupted by another ringing of the phone.

Brown reached for it and Lavagni went on toward the door, then he heard the black man saying, "Yeah he's here, just a minute."

Lavagni turned back with a questioning look. Brown was extending the instrument toward him. "It's your chief rodman. He sounds like his eyes might be rolling."

Lavagni strode back to the desk and snatched the telephone. "Yeah?" he said quietly. His face fell immediately as the receiver rattled with some breathless report, then he deposited the paper bag on the desk and reached for a handkerchief. "No, hell no, keep away from those cops!" he barked, dabbing at his forehead with the handkerchief. "After they leave, you go through there with a sieve. You make damn sure he's not hiding in a john or something. Then you get a rundown on every plane that left out of there during that time, and you get copies of the passenger lists . . . shit I don't care how you get 'em, just get 'em!" He deposited the phone with a crash and growled, "That bastard!"

"Bolan got away again," Brown decided in flat tones.

"That bastard!" Lavagni repeated.

"I can get 'im."

"Huh?"

"I can get Bolan for you."

"Shit!" Lavagni sneered. "You and what cock-a-doodle army? We got the whole goddam country swarmin' for that guy, and *you* say . . ."

"I can kill him with a kiss."

"Hey, I ain't in no mood for . . . what the hell you mean? You mean the Judas kiss?"

"Something like that," Brown replied quietly. "I did duty with the guy. I know him. I waded rice paddies with him and jungle-skunked 'im for about three months once. Yeah, I could—"

"Then why didn't you say so before?" Lavagni asked coldly, watching the black man through half-slitted eyes.

Brown shrugged. "I'm not no Maf—I'm not one of you, man, I just work here. And I didn't figure I'd get no popularity medals for knowing Bolan."

"Well that's a hell of a goddam attitude!" Lavagni shouted. "Now how'm I supposed to know what the hell you been up to, huh Wils? How'm I supposed to know what you'n that bastard Bolan've been cooking up, huh?"

The two black men near the door were moving nervously toward the disturbance. Brown shot them a quick glance and said, "It's okay." To Lavagni, he said,

"Just use your head, that's all. This ain't no confession, you know. I'm telling you I can get Bolan for you."

"Why?" the Italian asked suspiciously. "You're already my best right hand, right here. I admit, you been smart staying out of this other mess. So now why you stoppin' being smart, Wils? Huh?"

Brown shuffled uncomfortably and hunched his shoulders forward in a thoughtful stance. "Well, I been thinking. I'm not no part of nothing, you see. I'm just *me,* Wils Brown, and I'm whatever I can make for myself. Right? How much can Wils Brown make for himself, Tony, if he gets Mack Bolan for you?"

Brown had come up with the one convincing argument which Quick Tony Lavagni could understand, and with which he could identify. He was quietly studying the idea and scrutinizing his central controller, obviously seeing him in an entirely different light than ever before. "There's a hundred thou contract on Bolan," he explained slowly. "Arnie Farmer has added another hundred thou if he can get his hands on th' bastard while he's still alive."

Brown smiled solemnly. "Well now, see? Wils Brown would kiss Jesus himself to be a part of *that* purse, Tony."

"I got an interest in anything going in my territory, Wils," Lavagni carefully pointed out.

"Okay, I'd give you a split," Brown agreeably replied.

"And Arnie hisself, he's got an interest too."

"He pays out with one hand and takes back with the other?"

"That's business, Wils." Lavagni was deep in thought. "Like Uncle Sam."

"Yeah, same idea, like taxes you know. Okay, I guess

we better go clear this with th' farmer. Get your coat, Wils."

Brown grinned. "You gonna take me to the big man, eh?"

"Yeah," Lavagni replied, frowning. "But listen, you gotta be respectful. You can't talk to him like you talk to me. You call him *Mister* Castiglione, for God's sake none of this Arnie Farmer yuck, you hear?"

"I'll call 'im Mister *God* if that's what he wants, Tony."

"Awright." Lavagni suddenly smiled brightly. "Th' Judas kiss, huh? God damn, Wils, just wait 'til Arnie Farmer hears about *this!*"

3: Grounds for Deception

Arnie "The Farmer" Castiglione reigned over the entire Eastern Seaboard underground from south of New Jersey to Savannah, his empire embracing docks and fields, feeder cattle and packing houses, politics and labor, gambling and prostitution, and virtually all human endeavors which lent themselves to unscrupulous exploitation and manipulation. All this was ruled from the baronial estate known as Castle Farms in a lush Virginia valley not far from Washington.

Castiglione had suffered a painful thigh wound in the battles of the Miami convention[1]—actually, he had been shot in the buttock while scrambling up a wall to safety—and his mood had been something less than jovial during the following weeks. The wound was not healing properly. Soreness remained. He was required to sit on pillows and to inhibit his usual restless activeness. Every twinge of physical discomfort the Farmer experienced was accompanied by the pained growl, "That fuckin' Bolan!"—or, "Kill 'im, I'll kill 'im!"

Arnie had grown up in the concrete jungle of New York and had never realized there was a land out there beyond the pavements until he was nearly 12 years old. Now he prided himself as owner of vast unspoiled acre-

[1]*The Executioner's Miami Massacre,* Pinnacle Books

ages, a country gentleman and horse breeder. He rode in parades and horse shows, and his Appaloosa stock was considered among the finest in Virginia. He had found acceptance and respect in the genteel society of rural Virginia, and had served on various public commissions and was active in several philanthropic foundations. This was the image most highly prized by this self-educated product of East Harlem, and it was an image that had cracked and all but dissolved in the aftermath of Miami. Castiglione was one of the unfortunates who had been "busted" by the Dade County Force, fingerprinted and jailed and released on bail and still awaiting a court appearance on a variety of charges. Worst of all, his theretofore secret connections with the Mafia were being written about in newspapers and magazines around the country, and a Virginia crime commission had announced their interest in the Castiglione empire.

Yes, Arnie the Farmer had deep and lasting reasons for hating the guts of Mack the Bastard Bolan, any one of which could produce heat enough to roast the Executioner's carcass over an open flame. Arnie would gladly instrument the body to get a recording of every shrieking nerve down to the final death pulse, to keep and treasure forever and to entertain himself in moments of boredom. This very idea seemed right at the surface of Arnie's mind as he told Tony Lavagni, "I don't want this boy to die easy and alone somewhere, Tony. A quick kill is not my idea of justice, not where this boy is concerned. I want him dying slow and knowing it, and feeling it, and twitching around for a long time. You know what I mean, Tony?"

Lavagni assured his boss that he did know, and added, "That makes our boy Brown here a special case, Mr. Castiglione. So far we been lucky just to get a shot at the guy, but Wils here can walk right up to 'im, see, sort of get him off guard. We're thinking of a Judas kiss, Mr. Castiglione."

The Farmer winced and moved his wound into a more comfortable area of the pillow. "You've said that three times already," he reminded his Washington *Caporegime*. "I don't like that expression, Tony. I don't want you to say it again. Okay?"

"Sure. Sure, Mr. Castiglione."

"Okay." His gaze traveled to the huge black man. "This Bolan has had his face fixed. How do you figure to recognize him? How do you figure to make it like buddy-buddy with a guy you haven't seen since his face was fixed?"

Brown paused a moment before replying. He had developed an instant hate for the *Capo*. This cat didn't like being close to black men—a thick atmosphere of repulsion hung in the air between them. Brown squeezed his knuckles and said, "I'll have to play it cool, that's all. I've seen his pictures, I know about what he looks like now. If I can just get close to him, I figure he'll come to me."

"What makes you think that?"

Brown shrugged massive shoulders. "It just figures, man. This cat's all alone with the whole country after him. Can't trust nobody, can't lay his head nowhere and close both eyes at the same time. He needs a friend. I'm a friend. If he sees me, he'll come to me."

Castiglione was thinking it over. Silence enveloped the big open-beamed room of the fabulous ranchhouse. Brown's gaze shifted to the window, and he watched the horses moving lazily about the rich pasture. Those horses had it better, he was thinking, than most black men he knew. Then Castiglione broke the silence. He said, "Okay, but we have to work this thing out. You know, plan it—and I mean carefully. This Bolan is no punk, I guess we found that out for sure at Miami Beach."

Brown said, "I'll want a firm understanding about the reward money."

Castiglione replied, "How much you figure it's worth?"

"What is this, man?" the Negro said in an angered tone. "You cats already decided how much it's worth. You've spread the word all over the country, a hundred thou for Bolan. Now Tony tells me you added another—"

The Farmer said, "You won't deserve all of that. A contractor handles everything himself, like any businessman. He handles his own expenses, pays his own help. What's left is his profit. You understand profit. In this case, I'm the contractor. I'm hiring you. Now how much do you figure your part is worth?"

"Forget it," Brown snapped. He stood up and said, "Get me out of here, Tony."

Lavagni was staring steadfastly at the floor, unmoving. Castiglione sighed and said, "Sit down. It hurts my ass to look up. I see you don't like to negotiate. Take a lesson from a pro, Wils. Always negotiate, don't just rush off mad because the other guy says something you don't like to hear."

The black man replied, "Awright, I'm negotiating. I want the whole bundle, I want it all."

"You won't deserve all of it. We're going to back you, put up all the expenses, and that includes an army of rodmen. We're going to plan your moves, spot you, and work the setups. All that means time and effort and money. But we're fair, Wils. We'll split the purse evenly."

Brown smiled, sat down, and said, "Evenly means half for me and half for your backing, and it means half the total purse."

"I didn't say that," the Farmer smoothly replied.

"No, man, I said that. It's that or nothing."

Castiglione was smiling, but only with his lips. "You could get too damn big for your britches. They could turn to iron, and wouldn't that make for hard swimming in Chesapeake Bay."

The big Negro again got to his feet. "I been shit on by experts, man. I got over bein' scared a long time ago. Nowadays I just get mad and glad. Mad, I don't get Bolan for you. Glad, I'll give 'im to you in a gift-wrap."

Castiglione winced and shifted positions again. "That fuckin' Bolan!" he muttered. Then, "Okay, big man. We'll make you glad. You just make *me* glad."

"Half of the pot, net, for me."

"Yeah, yeah, you've made your deal." The *Capo's* gaze shifted to Tony Lavagni, who had been tensely silent and all but invisible during the discussion. "You got those planes pretty well nailed down now? You're sure of that?"

"Yessir," Lavagni replied. "There was only three possible ways out, by air I mean. Chicago, Atlanta, or Paris."

"You already said that."

"Yessir. I'd say Atlanta looks best, Chicago next. Paris would be a long shot. That plane was leaving when the boys got up there."

"Just the same we'll cover all three, and play heavy on th' long shot. This bastard always seems to . . ."

He reached for a cigar, groaned, savagely bit off the end, and clamped the cigar between his teeth, lit it, and leaned forward carefully to favor his wounded backside. "You know who we got in Paris. You handle it, be sure that plane is met, but don't mention my name in no transatlantic telephone calls. Understand?"

"Sure, Mr. Castiglione."

"Chi and Atlanta will be a snap. I'll put out the word myself from here. You get your boy here set up with a passport and . . ." He eyed the big Negro in a disapproving inspection and continued. "Get him to a fast tailor, make 'im look like a traveling buyer . . . uh, pick out something he knows a little about, something that would make sense him going to Europe in case it turns that way. Get him credentials and all th' crap, but don't use any of my connections, you know what I mean. And tell Paris to cool it. If they spot Bolan, just stick with 'im and let us know right away. Tell 'em anything you have'ta, tell 'em the contract isn't payable outside the country, just don't let 'em louse this up. I want a sure thing this time. I'll tell Chi and Atlanta the same thing. You just get this boy of yours ready to travel. You still with me, Tony?"

"Yessir, I'm still with you, Mr. Castiglione," Lavagni assured him.

The Farmer dismissed them. They let themselves out of the house and went directly to their car. As they were moving along the graveled drive, Brown chuckled and observed, "I never seen you so courteous and polite, man."

Lavagni growled something inarticulate, then replied, "Maybe you better try some of the same, Wils. Arnie Farmer is nobody to cross. He likes to be treated with respect, and you better watch the way you talk to him. Especially until he's well and back on his feet again. You put him over a barrel, you know that, Wils—and he don't like that a little bit."

Brown heaved a contented sigh. "He don't scare me none. I'll say this, though. I'm glad I'm not Mack Bolan. Man, I never saw so much hate, and I'm an expert on hate."

"You ever been to Atlanta, Wils? Or Paris?"

"Sure man, I been everywhere there is to go. And it's the same stinkin' world every place, huh."

Lavagni nodded his head. "I guess so. This Bolan's going to find that out too, Wils. There ain't no place he can go where we can't get at him. It might be Atlanta, it might be Chi, it might be Paris. But it won't matter, it's all the same. He's going to find that out."

"I bet he already knows it," Brown said, sighing. "He's been everywhere too, man. Everywhere but dead. Wonder what it's like there."

"Where?" Lavagni asked, throwing the black man a quick glance.

"Th' land of the dead, man. I wonder what it's like."

Lavagni chuckled and said, "When you're kissing Bolan, ask 'im. He's dead already and just won't admit it."

Brown slumped into the seat and gazed out the window at the fields blurring by. "Well, we'll just have to make it official, won't we," he said softly.

"Just kiss 'im, Wils," Lavagni said in a solemn voice. "That's the closest thing to a last rite he'll ever get."

"I'll kiss him with an amen then," the huge Negro muttered.

Bolan was at the self-serve coffee bar helping himself to an early morning refresher when the stewardess came in and told him, "Orly Airport in about twenty minutes, Mr. Ruggi."

He said, "Thanks," and wondered what else she had on her mind. She had not walked all the way back there simply to tell him that.

"Are you traveling with Mr. Martin?" she asked casually, confirming Bolan's assessment of her motives.

"No," he replied. "I'd never heard of the guy. Who is he?"

"Come on, you're kidding," the girl said. "You're his double, aren't you."

"Double for what?"

"Come on now, Mr. Ruggi."

Bolan relented and grinned. The girl was standard overseas-airline sleek, chic, leggy, with jet black hair, smooth skin—pretty, interesting enough for any man, the Gil Martins included. "How do you know he's not *my* double?" he asked, using a teasing tone.

She was not to be teased. Eyeing him thoughtfully, she raised a hand and fingered his sideburns. Bolan caught the hand and held it—this was getting out of control. "We don't really look that much alike," he said gruffly.

"Side by side, no," she replied, laughing softly to gloss the moment of tension. "But . . ."

Bolan said, "Drop it, please. It's not what you think."

"No, it's not," she replied, still speculatively eyeing him. "I had it all wrong. *He's* the ringer. I should have known, he's too blah. You bring him along to run interference for you, don't you."

The ex-GI from Pittsfield had not been trained for jet-set maneuverings; the man of him, however, knew that he was being rushed. The whole thing seemed entirely out of character for an airlines stewardess, in Bolan's view at any rate, and he was having trouble reading the signs. He gave her back her hand, forced a laugh, and said, "You're wrong all the way. Seriously. Would you like to see my passport?"

She shook her head, apparently deciding to ignore his protestations, and said, "Are you staying in Paris long?"

"Couple days, maybe."

Her eyes gleamed with sudden mischief. "Your double is going on to Rome, or so his ticket says."

Bolan said, "Frankly, I don't give a damn where he's going. How can I convince you—"

"Orly is my turnaround port," she said quickly. "I'll be there until Friday."

Okay, he thought, so the signs were becoming infinitely more readable. "That's nice," Bolan replied.

"I usually stay at the *Pension de St. Germain* when I'm laying over."

"Why?"

The girl seemed flustered by the direct question. "Well it's cheap and it's clean. And I like the St. Germain area. I guess you're a Right Banker, though—Champs Elysees or bust." She showed him a rueful smile. "On airline pay, it's the *pensions* or bust for darned sure."

"What's a *pension?*" Bolan asked, though he already knew.

"It's a boarding house."

Bolan said, "Oh."

"Not exactly," she quickly added. "They're family

type hotels. You get room and three meals for about 30 francs a day, and that's where all the action is, you know, Left Bank."

Yes, Bolan knew. "Thirty francs a day is cheap?"

She wrinkled her nose. "That's only about five dollars."

The game could go on indefinitely. Bolan decided to end it. "Yeah, that's cheap," he agreed. "Okay, maybe I'll try your Left Bank."

"Pension de St. Germain," she reminded him.

"Okay."

"I'm Nancy Walker."

Bolan smiled. "Sounds like a brand of whiskey."

"No, wine," she flashed back, vamping him with an ultra-feminine smile. "Heady, romantic, nice to the taste and absolutely no hangover."

She left him standing there, open-mouthed and reflecting that the Gil Martins of the world certainly had it made. He finished his coffee and returned to his seat, arriving there as the seat belt announcement was being delivered.

Bolan buckled in and watched the man across the aisle. Yes, he decided, there were certain superficial similarities—he could see how the stewardess could have been misled into her erroneous conclusion. Martin was a surly type. He had spent the entire trip absorbed in a paperback book, sporadically dozing, awakening, and grimly returning to the reading, then dozing again—totally anti-social and ignoring repeated approaches by the stewardess and the passenger alongside him.

Bolan suddenly grinned to himself, a vision forming in his mind. Maybe, for a short while, Gil Martin, who the hell ever he was, would know how it felt to *not* have it made. If Bolan could be mistaken for Martin, then why couldn't Martin be mistaken for Bolan? If the French *gendarmes* were waiting down there at Orly, with copies of those composite photos of Bolan's new face to guide them, there could be a real comic opera down at the customs gate.

Things could be swiftly set straight, of course, with no more damage than the ruffling of a celebrity's tail-feathers, but the diversion could be enough to get the Executioner into Paris. It was something worth hoping for.

Bolan's fingers toyed with his false plumage and his mind toyed with this new hope. It would be nice, he reflected, for a while to simply have it made, to play and laugh and luxuriate in relaxed human companionship. Not *that* much hope, buddy, he chided himself. That's Paris down there, not Oz or Wonderland. Your hands are alive to kill, not to lovingly stroke a pulsing female form. You're the Executioner, damn you, not the playboy of the western world. Yeah, but it would be nice. For a while. The Executioner in Paris, gay Paree.

Bolan abruptly flung the idea from his mind. That was *hell* down there, not Paris. Only the strong and the resolute walked through hell. He meant to make that walk. And exit standing. A war awaited him, commanded him. Goodbye, Paree. Hello, Hell.

4: Engagement at Orly

After a brief delay in the holding pattern and an instrument landing through a dense ground fog, they were down, and off, and streaming inside the terminal building, Bolan keeping Gil Martin in sight, sleepy-eyed inspectors amiably waving them on through Passport Control with not even a glance at the precious documents. Bolan could hardly believe it, then he did not believe it at all. An inspector stuck out a hand as Bolan drew abreast and said softly, *"Votre passeport, s'il vous plait."*

Bolan sighed and produced the little folder. "Okay," he said in as bored a reply as he could manage, *"Le voici."* He had not used his French for some years, except in the rather limited and infrequent brushes with French-speaking Indo-Chinese, but he was happy to be able to handle the small formalities with as little fuss as possible.

Gil Martin had been stopped also, Bolan noted with some satisfaction, and was not faring quite so well; he obviously handled French not at all, and an English-speaking inspector was being dispatched to the scene.

Bolan's inspector was smiling at him and comparing his face with the image on the passport. Bolan fingered the growth at his face and lightly commented, *"La moustache, les pattes, c'est un difference,* eh?"

The inspector chuckled and replied, *"Vive le difference, Monsieur* Ruggi. *Combien de temps comptez-vous rester?"*

He wanted to know how long Bolan would be in France. "A few days," Bolan told him. *"Quelques jours."*

The inspector smiled again and returned the passport. *"Bon visite, Monsieur."*

Bolan thanked him and went on toward the customs section. A porter intercepted him and tried to take his bags, insisting that he could smooth his way and save him money. Bolan declined, kept his bags, and selected a fast-moving line. The inspection seemed to be little more than a formality, with most of the delay being caused by the confusion of the passengers rather than by the officials. Bolan lit a cigarette and casually looked back for a progress check on Gil Martin. The look-alike had finally cleared Passport Control and was hurrying into the customs area, following closely on the heels of a porter who was carrying an overnighter and a matching larger bag. To an untrained eye, this was the status on Gil Martin; to Bolan's eyes, much more was developing. Martin was quietly and inconspicuously being surrounded by a crew of plainclothes cops who, even without Martin's knowledge, were maneuvering him toward one of the private inspection rooms. At the last minute, Martin seemed to realize what was happening. He balked at the doorway and raised his voice in an angry argument but was pushed on through, the door closing behind him and sealing in the heated discussion.

Bolan grinned and moved on to the inspection desk.

He declared 40 cigarettes and no booze, and was courteously passed through without inspection. At this point, he dropped the casual pose and began moving in an attitude of planned haste. That could be Bolan back there in that private room just as easily as Martin; he wanted out and gone before the error was discovered. He stopped at the Orly *bureau de change* and took on a supply of francs, then went directly to a ticket window and bought space to New York on a flight leaving later that day. Then he found the door marked *Messieurs* and went into a private closet, stripped off his coat, retrieved his gun and sideleather from the suitcase, and strapped it on. Next he deposited his luggage in an airport locker and went out to find transportation into town.

It was late enough that dawn should have been edging into the night sky, but the fog had thickened if anything and the outside lighting was making a very limited penetration and eerily illuminating the transportation circle. People were moving about here and there through the soupy stuff but Bolan experienced a feeling of isolation in the surrealistic scene. Something in the atmosphere there cautioned the Executioner and prompted him to step away from the entrance to the terminal, where the light was fairly good, and into the misty shadows beside the building. A crowded airporter bus wheeled through and disappeared. A suggestion of vehicles occupied a barely visible taxi station some yards up the drive; two private autos idled at the curb just below Bolan, their headlamps muffled and impotent in the heavy mists.

Then out through the lighted doorway strode Gil Martin, an angry scowl distorting his face. The same porter followed immediately behind with the luggage.

Martin pulled up almost within touching distance of Bolan and turned about to snarl at the porter, "Get the lead out! Get a cab over here, I'm not walking another step. I oughta go straight on to Rome, I shouldn't even go into this nutfarm of a town. I don't know what the hell I . . ."

The porter had silently deposited the baggage on the sidewalk and raised his hands in some sort of signal. Instantly another man came through the doorway and stepped up behind Martin; the American immediately ceased his snarling complaints and froze and a small leather case fell from his hands. One of the vehicles which Bolan had noticed earlier eased forward, a door opened and another man moved onto the sidewalk; then Martin was entering the vehicle and the porter was hastily throwing the bags into the luggage compartment. Bolan marveled at the smoothness of the snatch, aware that he had recognized it as such only when it was too late to intervene; the vehicle was disappearing into the fog, the second car following closely.

The porter returned to the doorway and bent to retrieve the small case which had fallen from the kidnapped man's hands. A foot appeared from seemingly nowhere to imprison the case on the ground—and when the porter elevated his eyes, he was gazing into the bore of Bolan's .32. He froze, stiffly off balance, and murmured, *"Que veut dire ceci, M'sieur?"*

Bolan said, "You tell *me* what it means, Frenchy."

"Je ne parle pas Anglais."

Bolan pulled the man upright and replied, "Then I guess I'll have to just shoot you and get it over with."

"No, I speak," the porter hastily admitted. "What is your wish, *M'sieur?"*

Bolan shoved him clear of the lighted area, scooped up the case and dropped it into his pocket, and joined his prisoner in the shadows of the building. He jabbed the little gun into the man's belly and said, "Who pulled that snatch?"

Something in the glint of the Executioner's eyes discouraged cuteness. The man sighed and his shoulders slumped and he said, "This is most dangerous, *M'sieur.*"

Bolan increased the pressure of the pistol and told him, "I'll take my chances. Are you ready to take yours?"

The porter sighed again. "So, they have the wrong man. *Non?*"

"That's it, and you have the right one. For about ten seconds, Frenchy, unless a flood of words changes the situation."

The porter shrugged his shoulders and replied, *"C'est la vie,* one is as bad as the other. I am not one of them, *M'sieur*. For two hundred francs I sell my honor and perhaps my life, *non?"*

"So who did you sell it to?"

"He is called Marcel. He is known for *les maisons de joie, comprenez-vous?"*

"Joy houses? Yeah, it figures. And where do I find this Marcel?"

Another shrug of the shoulders and, *"Les Caves, M'sieur."*

"The basement joints? Great, there's only about a hundred of them. You have to do better than that."

"I have seen him about *Place St. Michel."*

Bolan patted the man's pockets, found his wallet, and extracted an identity card. He studied the card, then slipped it into his pocket and returned the wallet. "Okay, I'll check that out, Jean. If I find out you're lying to me, I'll be looking you up. If there's something you want to add, now's the time."

"There is this *maison de joie, M'sieur,"* the man replied, sighing, "on the *Rue Galande,* near the point where *Boulevard St. Michel* meets the Seine. Marcel is known at this place. His other name I do not know. He is simply Marcel. He is known there, simply ask for Marcel."

Bolan cautioned the porter regarding the value of silence and discretion, then released him and watched him quickly disappear into the terminal. A moment later, Bolan was in a taxicab and telling the driver, "Take me to the nearest subway station."

"M'sieur?"

Bolan pushed his limited knowledge of the language into a hesitant, *"Conduisez-moi metro proche."*

The driver nodded and the taxi lurched forward, challenging the restricted visibility in a suicidal rate of advance. Bolan relaxed and put his life in the other's hands; he had decided some years earlier that Parisian cabbies employed guardian angels—and there were other considerations more urgently demanding and with an outcome not nearly so certain. Gil Martin had made no favorable impression on Bolan's mind. He had, in fact, formed a definite dislike for the man during that short flight. Nevertheless, Martin had obviously stepped into a Mafia trap laid for the Executioner, and Bolan could not simply stand by and allow another to suffer in his place—not even a Gil Martin.

He pulled out the leather case which had been dropped by the victim, and discovered it to be a wallet. Obviously the betrayed had been about to reward the betrayer, though certainly not to the tune of two hundred francs. In the wallet was Martin's passport folder, a wad of francs, an American Express credit card, and an identification card from American-Independent Studios in Hollywood. A newspaper clipping found in one of the pockets was praising Martin's role in a recent motion picture. So . . . the guy was an actor.

Bolan had never been much of a movie-goer, and he had never had much interest in screen personalities. He wondered just how big a name Martin actually had in the business, and how much of a fuss would be raised by his disappearance.

An actor. Bolan would like to see him act his way out of this mess. All the bluster and indignation in the world wouldn't . . . Bolan was staring dumbly at the wallet. The guy had even lost all his identification. The seriousness of the situation for Gil Martin settled into Bolan's bones like the cold fog outside. The name Gil Martin possibly meant no more to the French Mafia than it had to Bolan. What could the guy tell them—what could he say or do to convince them that they had the wrong man? One part of Bolan's mind was hoping that Jean the porter would beat it to a telephone and pass the word; another part feared that he would do so, and that Bolan was advancing into another drop.

Other questions bothered him also. If this had been New York or any other city at home, Martin would right now be lying in his own blood on the sidewalk outside the terminal. Were the Frenchies more cautious—less inclined to open gunplay? Or was there a deeper significance to the snatch?

Bolan leaned forward and told the driver, "Can't you speed it up? *Vite, vite!*"

In this fog, subsurface travel would be much quicker than the snail's pace allowed on the streets—hence

Bolan's desire to get to a subway. The Paris metro system was superb and easily transited. If Bolan could get to a metro station quickly enough, and if the information supplied by Jean the porter was straight, and if the abductors were being as hampered by the weather as was Bolan's driver—then possibly Bolan could pop up at the right time and place to save the hapless Martin from death . . . or from a worse fate. It was a wild gamble, of course, but Bolan's entire life had become a series of wild gambles. At least, he knew, he had to try. In the final analysis, Bolan realized, this was the last significant difference between himself and his enemies. He had not yet lost a reverence for innocent lives. To surrender that distinction would place Bolan in the same category as the scum he sought to eradicate—it would, in a sense, mean the loss of Bolan's war, the end of meaning, and another loss for an already losing world.

Yes, dammit, he had to try. He fished in his pocket and came out with the silencer for his revolver and attached it, then carefully tested the breakaway action of the sideleather. The driver was immersed in his impossible driving conditions, and was showing Bolan no attention whatever.

Bolan repeated, *"Vite, vite,"* then settled back in the seat and commanded his memory for long-dimmed details of the Paris layout. His last time here had been as a kid soldier on furlough from duty in Germany, and it had been a memorable two weeks.

Now he had come as a combat pro on furlough from some kind of purgatory, and he was not at all happy about being snatched back into hell again.

But if hell it was, then hell it would have to be.

He was not giving the Mafia even a semblance of Mack Bolan without a fight.

His destination was a house of joy. If Bolan had his way, it would quickly become a house of woe.

5: Executioner in Paris

Bolan removed his false moustache and sideburns and exited from the *St. Michel* metro station into a continuing fog, pausing briefly on the boulevard to orient himself. He was in the heart of the university district, not overly far from the Sorbonne and the Ecole des Beaux Arts. *St. Michel* was a wide avenue of sidewalk cafes and bookstores, though now practically lifeless in the early morning mists. He turned west and into a gradual uphill climb, then down *Rue St. Jacques* for a block and found *Rue Galande*. Here was even less life, an almost choking silence, a narrow and fog-enshrouded street of shops, old hotels, bistros, and a few basement dives affectionately known as *Les Caves*.

Bolan had been here once, on a pleasant spring evening many years earlier, and to a memorable *caveau* where a G.I. with limited means could nurse a single drink throughout the night and take in some of the hottest jazz east of New York. Warm memories stood aside for cold reality, however, as Bolan surveyed the now dismal scene. The fog had captured the odor of decay and too many centuries of living on the same spot—perhaps even too much dying . . . and what, he wondered, was really the difference? All of living was a slow dyingness, a gradual rundown of the clock of life, a decay-rate from the moment of conception. Violence, Bolan had long ago decided, was but a form of protest against that inexorable decay. Where the smell of decay was strong, violence somehow seemed a natural constituent also.

A chill shivered him and sent him on along the quiet street. At this hour of the morning, he knew the signs to search for, knew the telltale evidences of the form of activity he sought. The .32 came into his hand, the small weapon lengthened somewhat now by the silencer, and he walked quietly with the mists, themselves a dampener and softener and silencer of human activity.

A door opened somewhere up ahead and a woman's amused giggle entered the fog. Bolan crossed the street and moved on toward the sound of footsteps going away from him. A faint glow ahead halted him, and he heard the woman again, calling softly into the gloom a gay farewell.

He lit a cigarette and waited. Several minutes later, a repetition—the light giggle, a quiet male voice saying something in hushed French, footsteps on the walk, a feminine farewell floating out to send them on their way.

Bolan had scored. The signs were unmistakable. The house of *joie* was disgorging its overnight clients. This time the footsteps approached Bolan. He cupped his cigarette to shield the glow in his hands and pushed back against the front of a shop. A bulk moved past him and on along the sidewalk, the man moving hesitantly and feeling his way along the curbing. Yeah, he had scored. A few years back, the *maisons de joie* had been a natural and accepted legality in this ancient city of charm, and there would have been no standing room within them for a free ride by the Mafia, no opening whatever for the writhing tentacles of organized crime. Now *joie* was banned in Paris, the city of *joie,* and indeed the Mafia would find a fertility in that ban.

Bolan moved in closer and the next time the door opened he had a rather good view of the couple who stood briefly in the halo of light. The woman was tall and rather well put together. Black hair was cut short and curled loosely about the ears, a shimmering wrap of some sort belted at the waist, a nylon-clad leg projecting into the early morning cold. The man was middle-aged, well dressed, a soldier of the night. He murmured, *"Au revoir,* Celeste. *La soiree, c'etait formidable!"*

The woman's response must have been a prescription giggle, Bolan was thinking. It came the same as twice before, accompanied by, *"Au revoir,* Paul. *A plus tard,* eh?"

"Oui, certainement."

The man was on the sidewalk and moving away from Bolan. He awaited the final prescription after-call of farewell from the steps, then a swift movement placed him beside the woman. She stood there in a silently shocked reaction to Bolan's sudden presence, one hand on the door, the other clutching her silk-covered tummy.

"Bonjour, Celeste," Bolan amiably greeted her. *"Comment ça va?"*

Judging from the expression of dismay on her face, "it" was obviously not "going" too well at the moment. She shrank into the doorway, trying to put the door between Bolan and herself. He defeated the maneuver and moved inside with her. In the better light, Celeste looked better in the fog. Too much eye makeup and an overabundance of scarlet lipstick emphasized rather than softened the image of dissolution and too many years of horizontal trade. The body was still exciting enough, however; Bolan allowed that a darkened room would work about the same brand of magic as the fog.

They were in a tiny room which obviously had once served as the lobby of a small hotel. Two couches and several plain chairs overfilled the place. Bolan recognized the set. A stairway at the rear would lift to a larger, more sumptuous reception room which would, during the height of business hours, serve as a gay showplace and selection chamber for the wares of the house, and as a frolic center for refreshments and naughty conversation and perhaps a bit of dancing between acts. *Le chambre de soiree.*

At this time of morning, that upstairs chamber would be deserted and dismal, reeking of a mixture of alcoholic fumes and cheap perfume and perhaps even of expended passions. Passing through it on his way out, a guy would wonder what he had found so exhilarating about it a few short hours earlier.

Behind the lobby where they now stood would be the living quarters of the madame and maybe one or two of her pet pimps. It would smell like boiling vegetables and more cheap perfume, stale tobacco smoke, and dry rot.

Madame Celeste's eyes were flattened with fear as she contemplated the gun in Bolan's hand, particular interest going to the silencer. *"Chic alors! C'est sinistre!"*

Bolan said quietly, "I want Marcel."

"Non! Americaine?" She raised her voice to call out, "Marcel! *C'est l'Americaine!"*

Immediately the door at the rear of the lobby opened and a man of about 25 entered, a short but powerful looking Frenchman with a wide grin of welcome. The grin faded into uncertainty as he stared at Bolan, then another man pushed in behind him.

The second man got a good look at the visitor, yelped something in excited French, and whipped a pistol from the waistband of his trousers. Bolan's .32 phutted dully and blood geysered from between the man's eyes. He hit the floor dead, his pistol clattering across the floor and sliding to a rest almost at Bolan's feet. The first man was diving back toward the door. Bolan's second round helped him get there, the slug plowing into the back of the skull and dropping him in the doorway.

The woman called Celeste was staring unbelievingly into the scene, mouth open and moving but no sounds issuing. Bolan clamped a hand onto her shoulder and shook her. "Speak English," he commanded. "Who were they expecting?"

Sound came on her second try, rasping through a parched throat and a paralyzed tongue. *"Non, non,"* she choked.

Bolan let her go and she crumpled to her knees. A sound on the stairway whirled him about as a blonde girl of about twenty descended quickly into view, then halted halfway down in sudden confusion as the scene presented itself to her. She wore absolutely nothing but a narrow garter belt and thigh-length hose of black mesh. She cried, "My God! I thought I heard . . ."

Bolan growled, "Get on down here!"

She came down hesitantly, a voluptuous vision of pink skin and well-piled flesh, eyeing Bolan as though he were a cobra about to strike, then she scuttled quickly across to be near Celeste. She asked Bolan, "Wh-what is this? What are you doing?"

Her speech was that of a refined Englishwoman.

Bolan wondered what the hell she was doing in this lousy drop. He told her, "I'm not up on the language. Tell Celeste she has one chance to live. I want information and damn quick. Are they bringing the American here? How many of them are involved. When are they expected?"

A rapid exchange in French between the two women ensued. Then the blonde girl told Bolan, "Yes, an American criminal was to be brought here. He was to be kept here until further instructions were received. She does not know how many, she understood it was to be but one. Do you mean—oh yes, I see what you mean." She turned to the older woman and another discussion, then back to Bolan. "Seven men went to the airport, in two machines. She feels that they have been delayed by the fog. They should have arrived before now."

Bolan said, "Okay, that's what I wanted." Under other circumstances he would have wanted something quite different from the English beauty, but this was just another of the sacrifices to the lousy war. He told her, "Get the woman upstairs. Stay there. Don't let anyone else down."

The girl nodded her head in vigorous assent and pulled Celeste toward the stairs. The French woman was beginning to tremble and weep. Bolan watched them up the stairway, hoping that Celeste had not become overly attached to her dead pimp, and working hard to keep his eyes away from the invigorating display of blonde rump, then he quietly put out the lights, opened the door, and went outside.

The situation out there had not changed. The street was quiet and the fog was showing no signs of dissipating. Bolan took a position several steps uprange from the doorway, secure in the enveloping mists. He noted lights going on upstairs and supposed that the house of *joie* was coming alive in a premature awakening. He replaced the two expended cartridges in the .32 and settled into the wait, trying to not think of the English girl. Half a cigarette later, the sound of an automobile engine entered his consciousness, followed quickly thereafter by the slow advance of headlamps along the curbing—then another sound and another pair of lights.

The vehicles came to a halt just below Bolan's position. A car door opened, feet moved on the sidewalk, then both pairs of lights winked out. A nasal voice called, *"Depechez-vous!"*

Yeah, Bolan thought, hurry up and die.

Distorted shapes wavering in the gloom, car-doors in motion, a quiet murmur of voices—this was the area of perception. Bolan moved softly toward the entrance to the house. A lone figure approached, nothing more than a shapeless suggestion of mass. Bolan stepped beside him and caught him behind the ear with the butt of the gun, then grabbed the falling body and assured it a soft and soundless descent to the ground.

Three more blobs moving toward him . . . yeah, here was paydirt—the middle blob sort of bent and sagging and being dragged along by the other two. The .32 whispered two coughing little words, the two outside blobs fell away and the inside one tumbled toward Bolan. He caught it, hissing, "Quiet, quiet," and got an arm around it and guided it up the sidewalk toward Rue St. Jacques.

Behind them a troubled voice called out, "Armand? Henri?"

Bolan kept moving, trying to get as much distance

as possible before the light dawned back there. He saw the headlamps of the lead car flash back on and heard the sounds of aroused voices. The man beside him was breathing raggedly and trying to tell him something in a pained monotone. But there was no time for sidewalk conferences. Running feet were pursuing them up the sidewalk and the vehicle was moving forward again.

Bolan pushed his burden against the wall of a building and shoved him down into a seated position, then dropped to one knee and swivelled to the attack. Immediately the running feet became an identifiable figure bearing down on him. He squeezed off another quiet phut and the running figure pitched forward and became a sliding mass.

The .32 angled up and over, Bolan sighting in an imaginary target just above the dull glow of an automobile headlamp, and he sent three quick rounds into there in a right-to-left scan. The crashing of window glass and a sudden veering of the headlamps announced his success; the vehicle headed off on an erratic course, crossing the street to the other side and moments later smashing into an immovable object.

A man's voice was yelling something in a mixture of French and Italian, then the same voice rose in hysteria and was screaming for help. A sudden flash of light hinted at the fire over there, and then an explosion settled all doubts. Confusion and running about and excited voices down near the *maison de joie;* screams and hot flames piercing the fog at the far side of the street; female voices pitched high in excitement and floating down from Madame Celeste's balconies—to this backdrop, Bolan took time to thumb in two fresh rounds of ammo, then he reclaimed his charge and hustled him along the street as fast as he could move him.

They reached *Rue St. Jacques* as *Rue Galande* began bursting with curious life and all traffic seemed to be heading counter to Bolan's progress. He paused at the corner and allowed Martin to get his breath. Back there were leaping flames and excited people crowding about like wraiths in the weird glow. If there was a pursuit, Bolan could not see it—but then, he could not see much of anything. He asked Gil Martin, "Are you okay?"

"No," Martin groaned. "They . . . fiends. Fingers broken . . . and kicked, kicked, ribs burn."

"We have to keep going," Bolan told him. "Can you make it?"

"Yes. Anything. Th-thank God. Yes, go."

They went, moving quietly and surely along *Rue St. Jacques* and onto *Boulevard St. Michel,* Bolan beginning to develop an entirely new feeling about the quality of one Gil Martin. They paused again there, at the Boulevard, Bolan trying to orient himself as to present location and desired goals. A name that sounded like an American whiskey flashed into his mind and the inviting declaration re-whispered, "I usually stay at the *Pension de St. Germain."*

Bolan did not know the place but he knew the street and vaguely recalled the area of *Boulevard St. Germain* where budget hotels were prominent. For a guy in good shape it was within walking distance, but for his hurting companion . . . He guided Martin toward the metro station. If he remembered correctly, *Metro Odeon* would put him somewhere in the ballpark and he could find it from there.

As they approached the station, Martin gasped, "Why are we . . . running? Let's . . . find a cop."

Bolan replied, "We can't do that."

"Why not?"

"All right, change that to read *I* can't do that. Do you want me to leave you here, or do you want to go on my way?"

They had reached the entrance to the metro station, and in that light Bolan got his first good look at the kidnap victim. Martin's arms were folded across his stomach, crossed at the wrists so that the fingers could find support upon the forearms. His face was welted and lumped, one eye closed completely, the upper lip puffed and bloodcaked. Beneath the coat and inside the shirt, Bolan knew, would be found more horrors. The mob did not take kindly to the adventures of Mack Bolan. His voice was softly sympathetic as he asked Martin, "Well? Are you with me?"

The actor was staring at his benefactor with quiet gratitude. In his one good eye was a light of revelation as recognition flared there. He nodded and said, "I'm with you, Bolan."

Bolan smiled and helped him down the steps. If things should work out, the actor would be with someone else very shortly and a brassy-talking airline stewardess would have her chance to put up or shut up. And maybe she'd get herself a bonus layover, after all. But not Bolan. The Executioner was even then mentally committing himself to a hellish layover. He felt an attack of Mafia Fever coming on, an infection to which the sharpshooting sniper from Vietnam was most susceptible.

There were but two cures for it.

Death, or Mafia blood.

Bolan was ready for either.

6: *Dimensions of Death*

Bolan pushed the door full open and planted his burden in the doorway. "We need a bed, and quick," he told the startled girl.

She fell back into the room with a stifled yelp and allowed Bolan to maneuver the injured man to the bed.

The girl wore a terry cloth mini-sarong which didn't quite make it over jutting breasts and bottomed-out just below the hips. A small bath towel was wrapped about her head in a neat turban. She looked pink and shiny-scrubbed and a hell of a lot prettier than the airline uniform had made her. She fussed about with the pillow and guided Martin's head to it, then she turned to Bolan with a sick look and said, "Don't tell me he got that way hurrying here to keep a date you neglected to confirm."

Bolan muttered, "You still have it all wrong."

Her mood was visibly shifting from startled concern to one of marked hostility. "Oh no," she told him, "I have it all right. You're Johnny Charming sans face wig, and this poor slob has taken one too many dives for you. How does it work, Mr. Martin? You take the women and he takes on the infuriated boyfriends?"

Bolan read it that she had been smarting under her

own overplay on the plane, and was now letting him know that the game had changed. He pressed Martin's passport into her hand and said, "I tried to tell you that you had it wrong." He turned back to the bed and left her staring at the passport photo. He asked Martin, "How is it?"

"I'll live."

Bolan wished to make sure. He carefully opened the shirt and peeled up the undershirt with gentle hands. The guy's chest was one big blue-blotchy mess, with angry red bloodblisters spaced about. "They did this with their feet?" Bolan inquired. He was tenderly probing the ribs with sensitive fingers.

Martin grimaced and replied, "Yeah. The belly, too."

"Must've had steel caps on the shoes." Bolan opened the waist of the trousers and bared the lower torso, took one quick look, then shook his head and stood up. "You'll have to have a doctor," he told the actor.

"I'm for that. My hands . . . *God,* my hands."

Nancy Walker bustled in with a wet towel and began carefully dabbing at his face. She told Bolan, "Don't worry about him. I'll get the doctor."

He replied, "Okay," and paced nervously about the room for a moment, then he went back to the bed and told Martin, "I'll be leaving you now. Uh . . . guess I don't have to say it . . . but . . . well, I'm sorry for those lumps."

The actor winked his one good eye. "Lumps I can take. You just watch it, eh?"

Bolan said, "Yeah," and chewed his lip for a moment. He hated to leave the guy this way. *Mafiosi* could be persistent hunters. Sanity dictated, however, that he get out and let the guy have some medical attention. He dropped Martin's wallet on the bed and told him, "You'll be needing this. The girl has your passport." He spun about, stepped past Nancy Walker, and went toward the door.

"Bolan!"

He halted and turned back. "Yeah?"

"Maybe you better take that passport. You know?"

"No, I . . ."

"You could fake it out, you know that by now. And the French cops already have egg on their face over me. You be Gil Martin for a while and I'll take a rest. I needed it even before this."

Bolan hesitated, thinking about it. Martin was thinking in terms of cops. Bolan's mind was occupied with *Mafia*.

The girl was staring from one to the other of them, a quizzical half-smile prettying her face. She told Bolan, "I heard what he called you, and the message now is loud and clear. His offer makes sense." She tossed him the passport folder. "Trade. Give me yours."

"Take all the identification," Martin urged. "Money too, if you need it. Or use the credit cards. Just don't go wild, I'm not that wealthy."

A warmness was spreading through Bolan's gut. He had almost forgotten the feeling. It was damn nice, if for only a fleeting moment, to feel the touch of genuine friendship. On that note of warmth he traded wallets and passports with the actor, thanked the girl with his eyes, and got out of there. He figured the trade at about fifty-fifty, in terms of personal danger. Some of the mob had egg on their face over the Gil Martin mix-up also; others of them might still be sniffing along that false trail, and it was this consideration that tipped the decision for Bolan. If the mob came looking for anyone, he wanted them to find *him,* not some poor defenseless Hollywood type who couldn't even spell *kill.*

The more he thought of the set-up the better he liked it. Let Martin stay down and out of the line of fire, at least until the action had swirled away into another part of the world. When the time was right Martin could present himself to the police, explain what had happened, reclaim his place in the world, and relate a true-life adventure which would fill columns of free publicity for a long time to come.

As for the girl, she had a battered but very much alive movie star in her keep for a few days . . . and who could say how that relationship would ultimately work itself out?

Bolan returned to the metro and found his way to the glitter-side of Paris. As Gil Martin he checked into a large hotel on the *Champs-Elysees,* left stern orders as to his right to privacy, and turned over the key to the airport locker so that his bags could be picked up. Then he ordered a rental car, to be kept at his disposal in the hotel garage, and went up to his suite for breakfast, a lingering shower, and a tired tumble between the sheets.

As his eyes closed on Chapter One in Paris, the time was barely nine o'clock on the autumn morning of Bolan's first day in France. Already it had seemed a lifetime. The days ahead were to seem as epochs in that strange life-as-death eternity which had come to characterize the bloody pathways of Mack Bolan, the peoples' gladiator and high executioner—and now, in certain Parisian neighborhoods, *L'Americaine Formidable.*

Silent rage vibrated across the telephone connection as Quick Tony Lavagni awaited the verbal reaction from the man at Castle Farms. His fingers were going numb on the instrument and he had moved the other hand up to help support the growing weight of it when the cutting voice finally found words of expression.

"I thought I told you," came the hot-ice response, "that I just wanted him spotted and tailed. When did I tell you, Tony, that I wanted Bolan snatched and hustled off somewheres?"

"That was their idea, Mr. Castiglione," Lavagni explained in humble misery. "I told those jerks how to handle it, but they had to get ambitious. I tried to tell 'em this Bolan wasn't no ordinary number, but they just had to find it out for theirselves. I told 'em—"

"*Fuck* what you told 'em!" Arnie Farmer yelled. "Now you listen to me, Tony, and you make sure you get it right this time. You take that black judas of yours, and you take a crew—a full crew, you hear?—and you get your ass over there. You shake that goddam place apart and you shake that bastard loose, you hear me? And you bring 'im back here in one piece. Now is there anything hard to understand about that, Tony?"

"No, Mr. Castiglione. I got it."

"Great. I hope so for your sake, Tony. How many frogs you say bit the dust over there?"

"I get it about six or seven, plus one of Monzoor's personal crew—a boy name of Shippy Catano."

"Uh huh. And so how many are you taking with you, Tony?"

"I guess I better take at least a dozen."

"You shithead! Whattaya mean, a *dozen!* Now, Tony, listen to me! You ain't thinking! Don't talk to me any *dozen!* Listen, you get out here, you hear me? Bring Fat Angelo and Sammy Shiv, and I guess you better bring that nigger. A *dozen!* Listen, brains, I *want* that boy! You hear?"

"I hear, Mr. Castiglione."

"So get it out here, and I mean right now. We're going to plan this thing to the last step, and we're gonna do it all ourselves. No more Frenchmen, you hear? Those guys fight with their feet and fuck with their face, and I guess they must think with their balls. I don't want nothing more to do with 'em. You hear?"

"Yessir, Mr. Castiglione, I hear."

"You better be here in one hour."

Lavagni assured his *Capo* that he would, and grimly rung off. He turned to Wilson Brown with an angry scowl and told him, "Arnie Farmer thinks *he* wants Bolan. Listen, Wils, I'm up to here with that guy. It's come down to this, Wils—it's him or me. You hear me? It's him or me."

"I hear you, man," the big Negro replied, grinning. "But I guess you better tell it to Bolan."

"I'll tell 'im, Wils. You think I can't tell him? You think I been that long off the street?"

The grin left the black man's face as he followed Quick Tony out of the room. He was feeling a bit sorry for his boss. Lavagni would tell it to the devil himself rather than face Castiglione with another failure. Yeah. That Bolan cat sure better look out. Desperation could make a mean enemy. Wils Brown knew it. Wils Brown was an expert on desperation, man.

In Paris, a dream was in the process of crumbling, an empire which never had been was now in danger of never being, and Thomas "Monzoor" Rudolfi was an unhappy and shaken man. America's silent ambassador to France, serving the subsurface society, Rudolfi was a forty-five-year-old lawyer and American citizen. He had lived in Paris since the early sixties and was officially regarded by the French government as a broker and advisor to American business interests in France.

Rudolfi moved in the best circles of Parisian society, maintained a chateau near the city which was frequently the scene of lavish weekend parties, and he kept a townhouse within sight of the *Arc de Triomphe*. He was close to many highly-placed government officials and politicians, was on a first-name basis with various French industrialists and financiers, and was frequently seen at social functions involving the higher echelons of France's cultural mediums. A bachelor, his name at various times had been linked with certain female notables of the theatre, films, and the fashion world. Thomas Rudolfi, a blood nephew of one of the founding fathers of *La Cosa Nostra* in America, had found the good life in France.

His had been a career of frustration, however, all the foregoing notwithstanding. Monzoor was a man of little personal wealth or power in the family hierarchy, though he in fact orchestrated a wide variety of the syndicate's interests in this area of the world. The Mafia, in its worldwide operations, resembled a feudalistic monarchy with strong imperialistic leanings, with each feudal chief, or *Capo*, an autonomous imperialist in his own right. Foreign "territories" had been staked out, cultivated, and jealously guarded by individual American families—then welded together for mutual strength under *La Commissione,* or the Council of Capos. This council, naturally, was U.S. based—and this brand of imperialism was even more invisible than the behind-scenes maneuverings on home soil.

Thus there was no such thing, *per se,* as a French Mafia. There were local mobs, home-owned and operated, but finding cohesion only in the franchise-like manipulations of the American families of *La Cosa Nostra.* Some American families maintained direct representation to their French interests, but on the broader scale of international syndication, Thomas Rudolfi was the indisputable authority.

Thus, Monzoor Rudolfi's dream of empire. He was, literally, in the *Commissione's* diplomatic service, directly serving the foreign interests of the American Mafia in their internationally syndicated strata of "business." He was also lobbyist and payoff man, arbiter and counselor, a central point of contact for the various American families who were doing business in France, and a liaison between the syndicate and non-syndicated crime elements who plied the French trade routes. After nearly a decade of such service, Monzoor had established links and broad avenues of influence which, in everything but fact, had enthroned him as *Monsieur Mafia* of France.

His income was derived from a fixed percentage of business grosses, as determined by the *Commissione.* He was sternly forbade any "independent action" on his own behalf, it being generally felt by the Council of Capos that a conflict of interest could thereby arise. As fair exchange for this latter restriction, however, the *Commissione* provided their ambassador of crime with a substantial living allowance and expense account, enabling him to move about freely and effectively in the higher strata of French society and thus better serve the masters at home.

Somehow, though, for Monzoor Rudolfi, this was not enough. There was nothing in this arrangement for the soul of a man, nothing to placate that insistent little voice from the inner man that cried for self-realization and fulfillment. If justice were to be done, Thomas Rudolfi would be officially declared *Capo* of France. It was his due. Instead of all the wealth moving toward America, with only a dribbling percentage left behind for the man who had made it all possible, the profits should remain in France and let the driblets cross the Atlantic. For some years now the conviction had been growing in the Rudolfi breast that this justice would inevitably one day find its level in the natural birth of the Rudolfi Family of France.

But now, on this particularly gloomy Paris day, Monzoor Rudolfi was a particularly troubled man. From the window of his townhouse study the massive architecture of the Arc de Triomphe was just becoming visible in a dissipating fog. He had moments earlier completed his third trans-Atlantic telephone conversation of the day—one of those guarded, heavily coded, and utterly depressing dialogues which usually left him with a mild case of the inner shakes. This one had left him with the outer shakes. Not only his dream but his lifestyle, his image—indeed, perhaps his very life—seemed to be in some precarious balance which was entirely beyond his direct control.

So Mack Bolan was in Paris—so what? Bolan was an American problem. Rudolfi should have no interest —certainly no *percentage* interest—in this mad chase across the oceans and the continents, this vendetta on the blood of a cheap rodman, a lone madman who should have been squashed months ago but for the gross mismanagement in the American branches. If Bolan meant anything to France, that meaning could only be stated in dollars or francs.

Rudolfi had long ago come to think of himself as a Frenchman. He spoke the language like a native, had begun to think in French and to speak English and Italian with an accent. Under his dedicated auspices, the French territories had established a power that would survive the rise and fall of a dozen republics—and, *oui,* of a dozen *Commissiones.* So who was this Arnesto Castiglione to suggest that it was time for a change in Paris? Eh? Perhaps it would be closer to the truth to suggest that it was time for a change on *La Commissione.* Eh? *Oui.*

What could this farmer, with an army behind him, know of the problems of Paris? What could anyone expect of a *Capo* who was not truly a *Capo,* or of a family which was not truly a family? The Paris headquarters consisted of five brothers-in-the-silence—*non,* but four now, the fifth lay in the morgue, poor Shippy, a toasted marshmallow of blackened remains. Rudolfi's crew! Ha! Was this not laughable? And yet this Arnesto had vilified and ridiculed this tiny family of France for failing to accomplish what all the collective armies of America had failed to accomplish, the squashing of the cockroach Bolan.

True, the cockroach behaved as a lion. But France had heard less than one day of his roar. How could the farmer of Virginia be so critical of France's restricted efforts?

Rudolfi thought that he knew the answer to that.

Oui, he knew. He knew the workings of logic of these *Capos* who had once been common soldiers of the streets. Keep France poor, this was the plan. Keep France wholly dependent upon the small commissions from gigantic business deals, make her account franc by franc for each business expense and the most microscopic item of the operating budget. Keep Rudolfi's crew busy with decimal points and give them no time to dream of genuine empire. Let France continue to be poor and dependent upon the pleasures of the bloodsuckers of America. But ask her to risk all to capture Bolan, the Lion of America, the lion which all America could not ensnare, but let not France expect the reward which all America sought. Fail, then, and suffer ridicule and personal vilification.

The underground ambassador to France sighed and stepped away from the window—but not, he resolved, away from the dream—the image of the Arc de Triomphe lingering in the optic nerves. *Oui,* let that be the symbol of the lion hunt of Paris. France would triumph. If necessary, the budding *Capo* would descend to the streets and bear arms. But France would triumph. Let the foreign armies come, let the great white hunters descend *en masse* from the streetcorners of New York and Chicago and Philadelphia—and, yes, from the fields of Virginia—and let them prowl the *boulevards de Paris;* they would all go away empty handed and foolish-faced. France herself would bag the lion, and France herself would demand the reward. Let them try denying it.

Rudolfi was not without local power. He could command one thousand guns upon an hour's notice. He could command government officials, courts, and entire police corps. But this was not merely a contest of power. *Non.* This was a challenge to the *soul* of a *man.*

So, Thomas Rudolfi thinks with his balls, eh? He went to his desk, unlocked it, withdrew the prized luger with swastika inlays in the handle, tested the action, then picked up the telephone and buzzed the garage for his car. The dream, he had decided, was not going to crumble. It was going to grow. It would grow in the fertile soil of Bolan's carcass.

7: *The Hard Set*

Bolan awakened at shortly past three o'clock, showered again, shaved, and had lunch with a towel draped about his middle. The valet shop had freshened his suit; new shirts from the tailor shop hung beside it. He deliberated a course of action over coffee, then came to a decision and first donned the black skinsuit which had become an Executioner trademark. Another brief silent debate followed, regarding the .45 automatic and its sideleather. He had heard of a place where one might obtain more exotic weapons . . . He resolved the debate by checking the clip in the .45 and the spares in the belt, then carefully stowing the set in his briefcase. Then he put on shirt and pants, strapped on the .32, tested the breakaway, finished dressing, grabbed his briefcase, and went to the lobby.

The desk clerk sent for his rental car and gave him a note which had been left in his box. It read: "Welcome to Paris, darling. But why have you not called?" It was signed "Cici."

The smiling clerk was anxious to be helpful. "Mademoiselle Carceaux is staying at this very hotel, M'sieur." His hand was on the telephone. "If you wish now, I will ring her—"

Bolan grunted a blunt, "No thanks," and went outside

to await the car, his mind freezing around the implications of that little note. Sure, Gil Martin was undoubtedly known throughout Europe—why shouldn't he have personal connections right here in Paris?

Bolan knew enough about human perceptions that he had had no great qualms about masquerading as an American celebrity in front of those who knew him only from his films . . . but anyone who knew Martin in the flesh would not be deceived by Bolan's likeness.

So okay, he would have to get out of the Gil Martin cover with all possible haste. One day . . . he would try it on for one day . . . and even that might be pushing things beyond the limit.

The car was a small sedan of French make, ideally inconspicuous for Bolan's purposes. He drove directly to the *Opera,* encountering no difficulty in finding that Paris landmark, then onto *Grands Boulevards*—that great succession of avenues which begins as *Boulevard des Italiens* and progresses through several other names and successively poorer neighborhoods, yet flowing on as a single bustling avenue of movie houses, music halls, shops, and a thousand interesting flavors of France.

He passed the red-flagged Communist Party Headquarters and continued on through several intersections before coming upon the one he sought, then he pulled off the avenue and found a place to park the car. There he slipped on the large sunglasses and left the vehicle. A five minute walk and several requests for directions took him to a narrow and dismal street which had once served as a focal point for the Algerian rebels in Paris, one of few such areas on the Seine's right bank; most Algerians lived in the Latin Quarter.

He found the little *"couscous"* cafe, in which nothing was served but the native Algerian dish with meat and rich sauces, and a strong Algerian wine. He also found the right words, and was led into a basement beneath the cafe and an audience with a fat and fierce Frenchman who, for five hundred American dollars, provided him with a modern, light, and extremely efficient little *pistolet d'machine*—an automatic weapon capable of delivering 450 rounds of .25 calibre ammo per minute—complete with ammo, clips, and compact carrying case.

Bolan was aware that he could have acquired the weapon for less than half that price, but he was in no mood for dickering. He politely declined a bonus of *couscous* and wine, tucked the gun case beneath his arm, and returned to his vehicle.

Thirty minutes later he was cruising the area surrounding *Rue Galande,* site of the earlier battle at the *maison de joie.* The neighborhood looked much better in the soft sunlight of late afternoon but Bolan was not interested in aesthetic values. His mind was working in terms of cartography, street layout, building plan, and various battlefield considerations.

He acknowledged the strong possibility that *Rue Galande* held nothing of further interest for the Executioner, but it was also his only starting point. It would be here or nowhere, and he had decided upon here.

He made several passes of Madame Celeste's, then left the car on *Rue St. Jacques* and returned on foot to a small sidewalk cafe which afforded him an unobstructed view of Celeste's front door. He dawdled there over coffee for some twenty minutes, during which time there was no traffic in or out of the Madame's—a normal condition for this time of day. Then he walked down to a modest hotel directly opposite the house of joy and rented a room on the third floor, front. As a soft drop it was perfect—and he had an interesting view from there of most of the neighborhood.

The manager of the hotel, a nervous man of about fifty, explained to Bolan that he was extremely fortunate to have found such a vacancy—actually the house had been filled with a Swedish touring party until that very morning. A gunfight in the street just outside had unnerved his guests and they had checked out shortly thereafter. Actually, though, this was a very quiet neighborhood where such a disturbance was extremely rare, and M'sieur must have no worries concerning a repetition of the morning's disturbance.

Bolan thanked the man and assured him that he was not worried. He also asked a few offhand questions and learned that none of the establishments of the neighborhood had been involved in the disturbance, *non,* it had been merely a passing disturbance of the street. This suggested to Bolan a thing or two concerning the official protection being enjoyed by Madame Celeste; her house had not become involved in the police investigation. Bolan idly wondered just how high that protection extended. A veil of official disinterest would work as well to Bolan's favor as to the enemy's.

As soon as the manager left him alone, Bolan opened the gun case and assembled the machine pistol, attached and adjusted the neck strap, loaded the weapon, and placed it on the bed. Then he undressed, down to the black nightsuit, took the .45 rig from the briefcase, double-checked it, and buckled it to his waist. Extra clips for the machine pistol went into the belt pouches. He tried on the new weapon again, letting it dangle from the neckstrap in front of him, found this awkward, and readjusted the strap for an under-arm hang.

This felt better. He removed both rigs then and placed them on the bed, removed his crepe-soled sneakers from the briefcase and put them with the weapons, then went to the window to begin a patient surveillance.

It soon became evident that someone other than Bolan was interested in the neighborhood. An odd-shaped automobile, perhaps a Citroen, had taken up a peculiar patrol of the street below. Bolan clocked the interval between passes at an average of five minutes. The reversing directions of travel suggested a figure-8 circling of the neighborhood. He could not read *police* into that maneuvering.

At five o'clock other things began to happen. First a lone man of rather nondescript appearance approached the house of Celeste, went past for about ten steps, then crossed to Bolan's side of the street and out of sight. A light in the lobby across the way flashed on, off, then back on. Immediately the man reappeared below Bolan's window, crossed the street, and went into the *maison de joie*. Others had obviously been watching his performance; they began drifting in from both ends of the street, in ones and twos. Bolan counted eleven entrants, each of them fairly young and casually dressed.

The Citroen continued the patrol. Nightfall was approaching, lights springing on here and there along the street. The cafe trade was moving inside; bistro time was looming. Across the way, however, all was dark except for the dim lights of the lobby.

At a few minutes before six o'clock a light went on upstairs. The blinds were open; Bolan was looking into the upstairs *chambre de soirée*. A man appeared briefly at the window and then the blinds were drawn. Moments later a door at the third floor balcony opened and a woman stepped outside. Bolan could not see her too well in the failing light but he could see that her hair was touseled and she seemed to be doing a great deal of yawning and stretching. The woman then went back inside and a light came on, muffled behind heavy draperies. Bolan grinned. The *mademoiselles* were coming out of the sack; another working day was beginning.

Something was wrong, though. Some minutes later a young man approached the house, went hesitantly to the door, and rang. Madame Celeste appeared briefly in the open doorway, some sort of discussion took place, the door closed. Too early? The man stood there for a moment, then turned to stare across the street. Even in the dim light Bolan could read the disappointment there. The youth swung angrily away and went back the way he had come. During the next hour this same act was repeated twice, but with different callers. Meanwhile the Citroen continued the merry-go-round.

Bolan watched, pondered, and waited. Obviously Celeste was not open for business. But at least eleven men were inside that house. A private party? Hell no. The entire thing had an ominous smell—precisely what Bolan was hoping for.

One lingering far-out possibility cautioned Bolan and kept him waiting. Those eleven men inside *could* be French cops, planted early into a hard drop. The Citroen *could* be an outside patrol, and in radio contact with those inside. Somehow, though, the scene did not ring with cops. The thing reeked of a Mafia hardset, but Bolan was not yet ready to bet any cop's life on the accuracy of his intuitions.

The Executioner could wait. Patience was a tool of his trade. Often he had lain unmoving in a clump of high grass for hours with Viet Cong moving all about him. Once he had sat submerged to the chin in a rice paddy for ten hours awaiting an opportunity to fulfill his mission. The hotel room on *Rue Galande* was much more comfortable than a rice paddy.

As the night moved in, so did the Latin Quarter atmosphere. Small groups of students of both sexes paraded about the street, moving from joint to joint. Snatches of conversations, uttered in a dozen languages, drifted up to Bolan's drop, mixing with the distantly muffled rhythms of jazz and rock music—here and there a congregation in the middle of the street as groups of youngsters stopped to talk or exchange information—and the ever-present Citroen threading its way through it all.

At ten o'clock the other side began showing an edginess. The Citroen tooted its horn on a pass of the house and kept moving. Seconds later two men came out and moved down the street. Bolan watched them intently. The car came around again and halted beside the men. The driver got out and stretched himself during a brief discussion from the rear seat, then he reentered the vehicle and drove on.

The two men from the house crossed the street and into Bolan's blind area. A pair reappeared moments later, crossed back, and went into the house. Moments later another two came out and went the other way. This time Bolan saw the switch. A man swung out of a shop front just up the street, another crossed over. The four conversed briefly, then the two outside men went on to the house and the other two took their places.

Bolan grinned. A bottle operation, with the Citroen as kicker. This said something very definite for the identity of the crew. Bolan could not mistake that set. It was typically Mafia.

He decided to make his move while they were unkinking and stirring around. He buckled on the .45 and swung into the *pistolet,* donned the crepe-soled sneakers, and went into the hallway. A dim bulb near the stairs was providing the only illumination at that level. The sound from a television program drifted up the stairwell from the lobby. No other interior sounds could be discerned.

Bolan unscrewed the light bulb, allowed his eyes to find their adjustment, then moved silently along the hall to the floating stairway to the roof. A small door at the top was bolted on the inside; both lock and wood framing were ancient; perfect, if typical, and Bolan suspected that it was.

He moved on to the roof and stood quietly for several minutes getting the layout. A common rooftop served the entire line of buildings; this, also, he had gathered during his earlier recon of the area. There was no moon and no stars; the only illumination of the night was being provided by the dull castings of the neighborhood's artificial lighting. He moved to the rear of the building and found the rusted fire escape. A very narrow and dark alleyway below, a door standing open down the way, a line of garbage cans. He paused at a chimney outlet and lightly smudged his face with soot, then moved cautiously across the rooftop to the end building, a moving shadow in the blackness.

Bolan watched for the Citroen, marked its passage, and quickly descended the steel ladder. A quiet moment later he was on the opposite side of *Rue Galande* and ascending to the rooftop of that line of ancient buildings. Here the going was a bit different, the roofs uneven and roughly joined, occasionally a low parapet separating individual buildings.

He took his time getting the lie and sniffing the atmosphere for human presence. Halfway back toward his goal he came upon a heavily breathing man of about middle age, mumbling to himself and hanging out a washing of underwear and socks, that area dimly lighted from an open doorway. Bolan watched and waited as the man completed his chore and went inside, then Bolan went on, considering himself warned of clothesline hazards.

He was using his own hotel as a reference point. He drew abreast of it with utmost caution and settled down to another breathless wait. Ten minutes passed. Satisfied that he was entirely alone up there, he found the door and went to work on it. Several minutes of patiently restrained labor was rewarded by a dull snap; the door swung open, and the Executioner had constructed his avenue to another hell.

He spurned the creaking mechanism of the floating stairway and dropped lightly into the hall. Something moved down by the main stairwell. Bolan froze and became part of the wall. Muted light spilled up the stairwell from the second floor; six doors at the third level, slivers of light defining each of them, behind him, a window to the outside. Utter silence marked the third floor, except for soft music and an occasional murmur of voices from below.

Bolan allowed the minutes to drift on, then he began his move, working his way in inches toward the stairwell, swiftly transiting each light-defined doorway, until he could see the skinny man sitting quietly hunched on the top step.

The guy was either asleep or half-asleep. Bolan closed

the distance in one cat-like leap, seizing throat and mouth in the same motion, lifting the sentry clear of all reference to the floor, carrying him quietly back into the shadows and not releasing the throat-lock until the possibility of outcry was gone forever.

He deposited the remains in a darkened corner of the hallway and began his exploration of the third-level rooms. He did not score until the final try. Beyond the sixth door, a young girl with shoulder-length red hair was seated at a dressing table and applying a scarlet substance to puffy nipples with a make-up brush. She wore a transparent negligee and shortie gown; the gown was pulled down from the top to allow free access to the task at hand. Their eyes met in the mirror, hers widening in immediate alarm. Bolan whispered *"Silence!"* and moved on inside and closed the door.

Plump breasts popped back into the confines of the see-through gown and she swivelled about to look him over with a shrinking gaze. He asked her, *"Comprenez-vous anglais?"*

She shook her head negatively but whispered, "A little."

Bolan showed her the machine pistol and told her, *"Pour les femmes, non.* I have come for the men. *Je veux les hommes. Comprenez-vous?"*

The girl nodded her head and tried to say something in reply. The words stuck. She cleared her throat and placed a hand daintily to the side of her face. *"L'Americaine Formidable!"* she hissed.

"Yeah, maybe so. The point is, I don't want you girls getting hurt. *Cette blessure pour les femmes, non."*

She again jerked her head in understanding, but the eyes revealed confusion.

"I want you to get all the girls up here. Can you do that?"

A blank look, a hesitant nod, and, "You wish me . . . go elsewhere?"

Bolan was not certain that he was getting through, or that he ever would. He pulled her to her feet and told her, *"La femme Anglaise,* blonde, bring her here, to me."

Comprehension dawned. The girl nodded her head vigorously and replied, *"Oui,* Judy Jones, I will bring 'er."

Bolan cautioned her with a finger across her lips. He patted the pistol and shook his head warningly, then went to the door, checked the hall, and motioned for her to join him. They went together to the stairs. Bolan stood at the railing, pistol at the ready, and sent her down alone.

Sure, he was taking a chance. That was the name of the game. Getting a bunch of women, even whores, in a crossfire was not. He stood tensely waiting, safety off, hair-trigger tickling the finger. Then came a sound, a movement at the bottom of the stairs.

He stepped back into the shadows, merged with them, and took up the briefest yet hardest wait of the night.

In his own mind Bolan was settling once and for all that age-old question about the heart of a whore.

8: Maison de Mort

Monzoor Rudolfi sat stoney-faced in the rear of the Citroen. Beside him was the somber Vito Bertelucci, Rudolfi's strong right hand. Driving and alone in the front was a weary native of Philadelphia, Charley "Roller" Guevici, who was at the moment complaining of dizziness.

Rudolfi muttered, "Shut up, Roller," and opened the miniature bar in the armrest. He poured himself a brandy and closed the bar, ignoring the needs of his companions. His rear end was paralyzed and he had a headache and he had long ago began to wonder about the wisdom of this hardset. Bolan was not stupid enough to return to the scene of his crime; he would not push his luck that far. But where did one begin? If not here, then where? Also, if Bolan had a terroristic interest in the Paris operation, would he not use this same starting point for an extension of further adventures?

Rudolfi sniffed the brandy and tugged at an earlobe, then he turned to Bertelucci and said, "Try the house again, Vito."

Bertelucci grunted and picked up the mobile telephone, placed the call, and settled back with a gloomy gaze at his boss. He got his connection. "Roxanne?

Vito. Anything?" He listened for a moment, then spoke past the mouthpiece to Rudolfi. "We have company. Lavagni and crew. What shall I tell her?"

"Tell her to get Lavagni and crew drunk."

"Seriously, Tom."

Rudolfi sighed. "Tell Roxanne to escort them to the chateau. Give them the full VIP treatment. She knows." He glanced at his watch. "Tell her we should be there by midnight. Perhaps with a prize."

Bertelucci nodded and relayed the instructions through the telephone, then he hung up and sat back with a sigh, lit a cigarette, and resumed the surveillance at the window. Around and around they went, and where they'd stop, nobody would. . . He flashed a quick glance at his boss and told him, "I need to take a piss."

Rudolfi downed the brandy before signifying receipt of the request. Then he kicked the driver's seat and said, "The place on *St. Jacques,* Roller. I suppose we all should get out and refresh ourselves."

Guevici's eyes in the rearview mirror were grateful. "Yeah, Tom, this ring around the rosy is making me dizzy as hell. Of course if it was accomplishing anything—"

"Shut up, Roller," Rudolfi commanded. He did not like to hear his own doubts voiced. Bolan would come. He knew that he would come. An empire awaited that coming. A lion with a roar could not for long remain mute. "Go on around," he said suddenly, changing his mind about the stop at *St. Jacques.* "Stop at the house of Celeste. We will refresh ourselves there."

Guevici threw a delighted grin toward the rear seat. "Maybe me'n Julio can trade places for a while."

Rudolfi grimaced disgustedly and replied, "How can you change places with Julio when you have never bothered to learn the language, Roller? How can you command a French crew when the only words in your vocabulary are *deshabillez-vous* and *etendez-vous?"*

Guevici chuckled. "I don't even know those. What'd he say, Vito?"

"Take off your clothes and lie down," Bertelucci grunted.

"Well, I guess that would get me by in there, wouldn't it, Tom? Anyway, I got better words for it than that."

"Give me a word for Bolan," Rudolfi quietly commanded.

"Bastard," said Guevici, coldly.

"Remember it then. And here is another. Death. *Morte,* Roller, in French. *Morte* has two faces. Remember that also. It comes and it goes, at the same time. Make sure, when you are looking at the bastard, it is going. Eh, Vito?"

"Just let me look at the bastard, Tom," Bertelucci said. "You'll see which way it's going."

The car was slowing and pulling to the curb.

"I would give ten thousand francs for such a look, Vito," Rudolfi replied, sighing.

The monzoor was about to get that look . . . but it would cost him an empire.

The shiny blonde head moved up the stairway and into the shadows at the top. Her breathing lurched raggedly as the apparition in black detached itself from the darkness and arrested her forward movement. "My God!" she hissed. "It *is* you! This is insane! This is—"

Bolan tapped her lips with a finger and said, "Quiet. Take me where we can talk."

He could not see her clearly but he could hear the

uneven breathing of tight emotions, could feel the warmth of her and smell the delicate aromas of boudoir grooming, and he could not keep out the vision of that enchanting female body as he had last seen it. He followed her down the hall and into a dimly-lighted bedroom. He closed the door as she dropped to the bed and turned to regard him in a mixture of fear and female interest. She wore flimsy harem pajamas and velvet slippers, leaving very little to the male imagination, and Bolan had to look away from her as he said, "You know why I'm here."

Her lips moved woodenly in the reply. "I suppose it's obvious. But it's also insane. There are a dozen of them here, armed to the teeth."

"Don't worry about that. I want you to get the girls out before the fireworks start."

"But how?"

"What are they doing down there?"

"Talking, just talking. Julio won't allow any bedroom action, no drinking, no nothing."

"Who is Julio?"

"The head thug, I take it. Large man, about 35 or 40, obscene and violent. He's in charge. Celeste is thoroughly frightened by him. Her husband, Marcel, was—"

"Marcel was her husband?"

"Well, not really, but they had a warm thing going."

"What were you about to say?"

"Marcel was always the go-between. For the payoffs, I mean. He was mixed up in many other things, also."

"Celeste is paying mob protection?"

"Of course. Otherwise she could not stay open a night through."

"How does she feel about this invasion?"

"You mean this one, tonight? She is very angry. With you, too, Mr. Bolan."

"I see you found the name."

"Of course. It is all we have heard for hours."

"Okay, give me the setup. How many on the second floor?"

"Eight. Three or four more on the ground floor. Others are in the street outside, I'm sure of that."

"And the girls?"

"All right below, in the party room."

"Yeah, okay." Bolan was deliberating the possibilities.

The girl asked, "How did you get in here?"

"Same way I'm getting you out," he told her. "The roof. Go get the girls, but very quietly. It all depends on you if they live or die. I'll give you two minutes to get them up here, into something warm, and onto the roof." He was looking at his watch. "I'm making the hit at exactly 10:30. You'd better be clear by then."

The girl's lips had begun to quiver. As she moved toward the door she asked, "How about Celeste?"

"What about her?"

"She hates you. I wouldn't guarantee her reaction to your presence here."

"Does she hate me enough to die?"

"I guess not."

"Be sure she understands the choice, then. Have you decided how to round 'em up?"

"Something will come to me."

"Try this. The boys down there are probably getting bored as hell. Make an announcement of some special entertainment. You want all the girls upstairs to work it out. Gay, you know? Strip-tease or something. Can you do it?"

She was vigorously nodding assent. "Yes, that sounds good." She hesitated in the doorway and turned back to whisper, "Mr. Bolan, it would be such an insane waste if . . ." She gazed at him for a brief moment, leaving the statement incomplete, then spun out the door and along the hall.

Bolan followed her to the stairwell and again took position in the shadows. Moments later a burst of excited chatter sounded from below. The young redhead was the first one up. She brushed against Bolan and whispered, *"Merci,"* and ran along the hallway. Apparently she had spread the word to the girls while Bolan was talking to the English girl. All were now racing up the stairs in a pretty good show of giggling excitement, but brushing by Bolan with whispered thanks.

Bolan was counting them through and, when Celeste and Judy appeared, he said quietly, "You two make ten. Is that all?"

The blonde girl replied, "Yes. Give us a minute to get our coats."

Celeste gave him a hard look and pressed on by. This was one of the things Bolan hated about his work. He wondered how many other sad widows lay in the Executioner's shadow, but he flung the idea from his mind and steeled himself for what lay just ahead.

The roof stairway was creaking into place. Soft-footed women were wrestling with coats and quickly departing the battle zone. All but one. Celeste stood at the bottom of the stairway and gazed toward Bolan.

She thinks I'm going to get it, Bolan decided. She wants to see me get it.

It was time. He moved the safety release on the

pistolet rapidly back and forth, assuring no failure, then went quickly down the stairs in a soft descent.

Three men relaxing lazily on a couch directly across the room took his first burst, the drumfire punching them deeper into the cushions as they gawked at him.

Two men at the window spun into the next burst, one of them crashing head-down into a nearby corner, the other going through the window in a shower of glass.

Bolan's death whirl continued unchecked. A bearded Frenchman in a beret, clawing gunleather, jerked his trigger prematurely and shot himself in the belly. Bolan added several more rounds for good measure, and whirled on.

Two men near the stairway had come unfrozen and had guns in hand, firing in a trigger-jerking frenzy at the fastmoving target. Bolan zippered them from right to left, then from left to right, and had to dodge back to avoid their falling bodies. He was feeding a fresh clip to the machine-pistol as he stepped over them and leapt down the stairs to the ground level.

Bare seconds had passed since the first eruption of gunfire. Two rather large men were jammed together in the doorway to the living quarters, both trying to get through at the same time. A gun hand was clear, though, and swinging on Bolan as he sent his own emissaries into the jam, and it dissolved and oozed to the floor.

Moving figures flashed beyond the doorway and a soft male voice inside was crying, "Julio! Julio!"

Bolan sent a figure-8 burst through the doorway and whirled to meet a challenge from the street door. A small man with a wolfish Italian face was poised there, gun cooly raised and spitting and trying to track onto

Bolan's movements, the slugs chewing wood behind the elusive target. A raspy voice on the other side was commanding, "Down, Roller, down!"

Bolan helped Roller down, with a zipper across the face that punched him back out the door and sprawling backwards onto the sidewalk. A whistling slug literally parted Bolan's hair as he rolled toward the sound of the raspy voice, and as he came up to the new attack Bolan recognized the big man behind the roaring .45. It was Vito Bertelucci, once a rodman with the old Capone mob and lately missing from American Mafia circles. Bolan made it a permanent absence with a target grouping tightly about the heart. Vito went down without a sound, dead before the fall.

The Executioner stepped quickly to the front door and discharged a short burst into the air, wishing to discourage any rush from that direction but reluctant to spray indiscriminately into the street. Then he went to the other doorway and stepped into Madame Celeste's private quarters.

A well-dressed man sat there, on the floor, staring at him. He held a fancied-up luger in a bleeding hand. "Bolan," he whispered.

"That's right." Another man lay close by, face down in blood, breathing with a bubbly sound. "It seems to be down to you and me."

The luger fell away and the soft voice announced, "I surrender."

"That's nice." Bolan could not help being struck by the ludicrousness of the situation. In all his lifetime of warfare, he had never heard those words.

"Look, I'm a businessman, not a street soldier."

"I guess you're going to die like one." Bolan went on into the room and placed the muzzle of the pistol against the man's head. It was hot. Hide fried, but the terrified man did not move so much as an eyebrow.

"Don't kill me, Bolan. Deal, I'm a businessman, let's deal."

"Okay, start dealing. But damn quick."

"You don't want Paris. No action here, Bolan. The action is south, the Mediterranean—Marseilles, Nice, that's the center of action. Evil action, Bolan, your kind of stuff. Narcotics, gun running, white slavery, all of it. That's where you want to be. Not here, not in Paris."

"Who the hell are you?" Bolan asked, curious.

"I'm Tom Rudolfi. You don't know that name? I'm the Ambassador to France, Bolan."

"Sure," Bolan said. "I haven't heard any deal yet, Rudolfi. You have ten seconds, then I have to be splitting."

"Names, Bolan. I'm giving them to you. Aumond, de Champs, Silvaterri. The big three, Bolan. South. Go south."

Bolan said, "Yeah," and slapped Rudolfi's skull with the muzzle of the pistol. The man sagged forward. Bolan stared at him for an indecisive moment, made a face, and went out. A guy was coming in from the street, saw Bolan, and flung himself back outside. Bolan grimaced and threw a short burst that splintered the doorjamb, then he sprinted up the steps.

He glanced at his watch as he ran through the chamber of death; the timing was great; hardly more than two minutes had elapsed since the first shot.

Madam Celeste stood stiffly at the third floor landing. Bolan paused beside her and murmured, *"Je regrette, Celeste, je beaucoup regrette."*

The woman spit at him. Bolan went on to the roof.

Only the blonde Englishwoman was there to greet him. She said, "I don't believe it."

"I do," Bolan replied, moving on across the rooftop.

The woman was trotting along beside him. He asked her, "Where do you think you're going?"

She told him, "You don't think I'm going back to that death house."

"Where'd the others go?"

"I don't know. They just . . . disappeared."

"You thinking of going with me then?"

"Well . . . I don't know where to go. The police . . ."

"Yeah, there's always that, isn't there." Bolan slowed his pace and steered the girl around the clothesline area. Back across the rooftop, a shadowy figure and then another moved through the lighted doorway atop Madame Celeste's. The pursuit was on. Bolan took the girl's arm and hurried her along. The weird sound of French sirens seemed to be homing in from all directions. They reached the steel ladder of the end building and he told her, "Quickly, down."

She said, "I-I don't know if I . . ."

The sounds of running feet were moving across the rooftop. Bolan heard a gurgle and a *whoomp* that could only mean a neck on a clothesline. Someone out there in the darkness was swearing softly and with great feeling.

The girl's hand was clutching his with a spasm of fear. He told her, "If you're going with me, Judy, it's now or never. The hounds are loose."

She threw her leg across the parapet and lowered herself over the side, eyes wide on Bolan. He followed quickly behind her.

Thus far the mission had been a huge success. He

had blitzed a Mafia hardsite and come away alive, with perhaps an item or two of useful intelligence and, for the first time ever, a soft bundle of spoils.

Now, if he could just make it back across a narrow area of hostile territory, maybe after all there would be a moment or two of R&R in gay Paree. But the Executioner was not setting any plans along that line. The Executioner had learned to live one heartbeat at a time.

9: The Paradox

Bolan was standing at the window and watching the activity in the street. The blonde girl was seated on the bed, legs drawn up to her chest, head resting on the knees. Her breathing was almost normal again as she told Bolan, "This is like a nightmare."

"Then I guess I live in one," he replied without turning around.

"Why?"

He shrugged his shoulders and kept his eyes on the street. "The French police are very efficient, aren't they? They'll be coming up here soon. I'll have to ask you to strip. This will have to look very convincing."

"Yes, of course. But you didn't answer my question. Why do you feel compelled to live this way?"

The street was alive with police. It was sealed at each end, numerous vehicles choking the narrow thoroughfare just below Bolan, men moving energetically all about. Bolan was grateful for the potentially hazardous haven just above it all; he knew that he would have not made it two blocks from the scene, not through all that down there.

He stepped away from the window and turned to the girl. She was removing the pajama blouse. He told her, "I don't know any other way to live. It's like fighting

Charlie, I guess. No clear reason for keeping it going, yet no safe and sane way to break it off."

"You didn't have to come back here," she quietly argued. She dropped onto her back and extended her feet toward Bolan. "Pull, please."

He pulled the pajama pants away from her and solemnly surveyed the nakedness spread before him. "You're lovely," he told her.

"Thank you."

He stepped away from the bed and removed his skinsuit, quickly folded it, and stowed it in the briefcase with the hardware, then locked the case and set it in the closet. When he turned back to the girl she was watching him with a calculating gaze.

She threw back the bedcovers and told him, "You're lovely too."

Bolan stood beside the bed and pulled her into his arms. "I warned you, we have to make it look convincing."

"No problem there," she murmured, and pressed into an entirely convincing kiss. They went down together in the embrace. The girl got an arm loose and pulled the covers over them. She giggled something incoherent and wriggled against him.

Bolan broke off and moved away. "Not that convincing," he protested.

"Then you'd better think of something to talk about," she warned him.

"Hell," he said.

"I suppose you're wondering about me. That is, about *my* . . . activities."

"None of my business," he assured her.

"I'm a writer."

"Congratulations. Direct research, eh?"

"Not exactly. Call it direct living. After years and years of schooling, I found that I had learned all the clever ways of saying things, but that I had nothing to be said."

"Yeah." He took her hand off his hip and held it. This was certainly the most unlikely conversation of his unlikely life.

"You don't believe a word of it, do you?"

"Does it matter?"

"Yes. I didn't come to Paris for . . . for *this*. I mean . . . prostitution. I came to taste life."

"How's the taste?"

"Horrible. And, at the same time, wonderful. You should understand, though. In Paris, prostitution isn't . . . well, it's not all that . . . well, many girls in Paris supplement their income in this manner. But it's dangerous for amateurs . . . in many ways, only one of which is the police."

"And Celeste offered you protection."

"Yes. I'm a . . . an extra. Well dammit! Whether you approve of it or not, it's the most logical way for a foreigner in Paris to keep from starving. At least this way I am free to come and go as I please. No one man is keeping me, I owe nothing to anyone."

Bolan smiled. "Hey, I'm no one to judge."

"Yes, that's true, isn't it."

He told her, "Some day you can write *The Confessions of J*, or something."

"Yes, and I'll get filthy rich."

"Your name isn't really Jones, is it?"

"No."

His smile broadened. "Pen name, eh?"

"No." She giggled. "*Bed* name."

Bolan started to say something in the same light

vein, then he checked himself and his eyes tracked to the door. He whispered, "Okay, this is it."

The girl had heard not a thing but moments later knuckles rapped lightly on the door and the voice of the hotel manager softly called, *"Monsieur* Martin?"

Bolan counted to five, then gruffly replied, "Hey, dammit, do not disturb! Can't you read your own damn signs?"

"Excusez-moi, Monsieur. The police wish to enter."

"Goddammit, you told me this was a quiet hotel!"

"M'sieur—s'il vous plait. The police—"

Bolan yelled, "Go to hell!"

A key turned in the lock, the door swung open, and Bolan raised belligerently to a seated position on the bed. The girl came up to an elbow and drew the covers about her shoulders. From the hallway the manager spluttered, "A thousand pardons, *M'sieur* Martin."

A plainclothes cop stepped cautiously into the room, then another. They gazed around, glanced skitteringly at the couple on the bed, then said something in rapid French to the manager. He advanced into the room and told Bolan, "There 'as been another shooting, *M'sieur.* The police desire to question you. They do not speak the English. I will translate."

Bolan growled, "You translate their asses right out of here! The American consul will hear about this, you bet on it!"

One of the detectives had gone to the window. The other was standing rather uncomfortably at the foot of the bed, darting quick glances at the girl. The one at the window said, *"Passeport, s'il vous plait."*

"And what if I don't please?" Bolan replied sulkily.

"Passeport!"

Bolan told the manager, "Inside coat pocket, in the—

I'll get it." He threw back the covers and swung his feet to the floor.

The detective quickly waved him back. "I speak English," he told Bolan. "Never mind the passport. We regret this invasion of your privacy, *Monsieur*, *Madame*. Just a few questions, please, and we will leave you alone."

Bolan said, "Fair enough."

"You heard the shooting, of course."

"We heard *some*thing. Little while ago. By the time I got up to look, it was all over. We, uh, weren't really interested . . . *comprenez-vous?*"

The detective's lips moved in a suggestion of a smile and he replied, "Yes, I understand. You saw nothing, then?"

Bolan's eyes flashed deliberately to the girl. "Inspector," he said in a confidential tone, "I wouldn't have seen King Kong if he'd been climbing in my window."

The corner had obviously been turned. Several routine questions followed, obviously of the breakaway variety, and the police made a graceful retreat.

The door closed behind them and the girl let out her breath in a soft whoosh. "They did not speak directly to me once," she whispered.

"Homicide cops," Bolan explained. "You have to understand the French. See no evil, know none, that's the philosophy. They didn't want to get sucked into a morals case. That's why he didn't look at my passport. He knew the manager already had. He would have been required to ask for yours, too, and he might have learned something he didn't want to know about."

"Then you handled it beautifully," she told him.

"Thanks. There simply was no other way."

"You handle all things beautifully, don't you?"

"I try."

"How are you going to handle this?"

"This what?"

"Well . . . here we are, aren't we?"

Yes, there they were. Bolan took her in his arms and told her of that very special sanctuary found only in a woman's embrace. She explained to him the very special difference between professional love and the spontaneous variety. Together they found that human bond that temporarily erases anxieties, placates mortal fears, and reaffirms the joys of being alive and young and together. And some time later, when their stories were fully told, she was lying languidly on the disarrayed bed and watching him with half-closed eyes as he quietly got into his clothes.

"Yes, you handle things beautifully," she murmured.

He told her, "That isn't hard when you're handling beautiful things."

"Mack . . . don't waste yourself on an insane war."

"It isn't insane," he replied. "You said something about tasting life, Judy. Listen . . . I don't know about women . . . but a man hasn't begun to live until he's found something to die for."

"I . . . guess I understand that. And I think I'm . . . ready to try my novel again, Mack."

He smiled at her, his teeth gleaming in the subdued light. "I'm glad to hear that." He went to the closet for the rest of his things.

"It isn't going to be *The Confessions of J,* either."

Bolan placed his gear at the door and went over to kneel at the bed. He kissed her lightly on the lips and said, "No?"

"No. I think I shall call it *No More To Die.*"

"What's that mean?" he asked, smiling solemnly.

"I don't know, except that I've been dying for years, and for no good reason whatever. I suppose I'll have to write the book to find out what it means."

He kissed her again and quickly stood up. "You'll find out," he said gruffly.

"Do you realize how very profound you are, Mr. Bolan? You've found the mystical secret of paradoxical logic. You *are* truly alive, aren't you?"

He went to the door without replying, opened it, picked up his things, then said, "*Au revoir*, Judy."

"Don't say that. Say *a tout a l'heure*—see you later."

"I hope so," he said.

"Me too," she whispered.

He went out and down the stairs and onto the street. It was shortly past two o'clock. All was quietly deserted out there now. He went up the street without challenge, got into his car, and headed for *Champs d'Elysees*.

Sure, he was truly alive. A man who lives in the constant shadow of death is always very much aware of being alive. He knew nothing of paradoxical logic or the strange workings of psyche that led a refined English girl into French *joie* service, but he did know that he had made a possibly fatal mistake of weakness back at that house of death.

He had left a survivor. He had humbled the guy and allowed him to beg for his life, then compounded the shame by walking away and leaving him alive. No man who was tough enough inside to survive in the world of Mafia could live for long with that kind of humiliation eating at him. The Rudolfi guy would have to vindicate his own aliveness now. He would have to answer to his own high priest of human pride and manliness, and the reply would undoubtedly be along the lines of what the English girl had termed paradoxical logic. Rudolfi would have to kill because he regarded himself as unfit to live. Of such questionable fodder were born the world's holy wars. Bolan understood this. Rudolfi would have to kill Bolan, or else lose his own right to live. This type were the enemies who mattered. Bolin understood this, also.

He only partially understood the English girl, God love her. Searching for her soul in a French whore house! He tried to relate her search to his, but quickly gave it up as a hopeless intellectual exercise. He quite frankly did not understand the female mind. Women lived for different reasons than men. They were nest-builders, civilizers. Even in prostitution they labored toward an affirmation of life, consciously or not.

Bolan, too, affirmed life—but in that paradoxical way. His supreme affirmation would be in his own death—and that awaited him around every corner.

He sighed and tried to bring his mind out of the depths into which it had been plunged by the set-to with Judy Jones. He sent the little car along *Quai Voltaire* and across the Seine at *Pont du Carrousel,* then swung up *Quai des Tuileries* past *La Place de la Concorde* and onto the *Champs.*

The skies had cleared, traffic was extremely light, and he found himself enjoying the quiet drive through early-morning Paris. It was with a feeling approaching regret that he pulled into the hotel garage.

He left the car with a sleepy-eyed attendant and took the elevator directly to his floor, bypassing the lobby, and was thinking of the contrast between left-bank and right-bank Paris as he entered his suite. It was like two separate worlds. With all this luxury, he was thinking, the crumbling little hotel on *Rue Galande* had held something for Bolan that all this elegance could not supply. He went into his bedroom and switched on the light—and abruptly changed his mind regarding *Champs d'Elysees* accommodations.

The girl in his bed was wearing nothing at all from the waist up. What he could see was solid elegance, and he could guess about the other areas. She sat up abruptly and held her arms out to him, her eyes straining for an adjustment to the sudden light.

"Gilbear," she crooned in a gently chiding tone, "I 'ave wait all night for you."

Oh hell, Bolan told himself.

Her eyes found the adjustment they sought. She did a startled little double-take at Bolan and jerked the sheet up to cover the delectably bare torso.

"But you are not Gilbear," she quietly decided. "And so, 'oo are you?"

Oh double hell, Bolan thought.

And he was not using paradoxical logic.

10: New Parameters

The chateau at the edge of Paris was ablaze with lights, but there were no sounds of revelry in the big house this night. A large charter bus was parked in the circular drive; groups of heavily dressed men walked restlessly about the lighted grounds or stood in quiet circles and spoke of solemn things.

Inside, in a large game room with a cathedral ceiling, Tony Lavagni perched atop a bar stool conversing in low tones with a statuesque French woman, the lovely Roxanne Loureau—confidential secretary and mistress to Thomas Rudolfi—a charming woman whose good breeding showed in her every gesture.

Gathered about a billiard table but obviously not overly interested in the game were five of Arnie Castiglione's most trusted hardmen. Each of these captained a crew of ten guns, all of whom had been personally handpicked by Castiglione himself.

This was a no-nonsense company of pros which had descended upon the Republic of France. The dismay and cold fear which lurked in the depth of Roxanne Loureau's eyes revealed that she, too, recognized this truth. Speaking in precise English, she told Lavagni, "I am certain that Mr. Rudolfi will be along most any minute now, Mr. Lavagni. But perhaps it is unreasonable to expect you to wait longer. Perhaps you would like to get some rest and—"

"The night's shot already," Lavagni growled. "Look, we didn't just drop in for protocol purposes. I need to make sure that Monzoor's covering us—I mean, you know, official-wise."

"But I have given you the necessary papers."

Lavagni grinned at her. "It takes more than that, and you know it. We want the right words in the right places, so's we can all go home when the job's finished. I ain't leaving no boys of mine in no bastille."

The woman was gazing at a list of names in her hand. "If they all are here, then have no worry. They will be protected."

Lavagni said, "I'd like to hear Monzoor tell me that."

"It is the same that I have told you."

Lavagni could almost believe it. This was a woman to be respected. He was telling her, "Just th' same, I'd like—" when the screech of tires on the drive diverted his attention. He slid off the stool at the same moment that the huge Negro, Wilson Brown, stepped in from outside.

"This must be him," Brown rumbled.

A Ferrari sports car had lurched to a halt just beyond the door. Rudolfi got out and stood beside it, gazing speculatively at the tour bus. He left the Ferrari's door standing open and walked around for a look at the front of the bus, then entered the chateau through the main entrance.

Roxanne excused herself and went through the passageway to the entrance hall. She reacted visibly at sight of Rudolfi. His right hand was bandaged and his hat was pushed back to clear the forehead where an angry circular blister marred the handsome features. Some sort of medicated ointment had been applied to the burn, only adding to the ugliness of it. Silently Rudolfi removed the hat and gave it to the woman. A small area of scalp atop his head had been shaven clean and an adhesive bandage applied there. His eyes were wild.

Roxanne asked no questions, but announced, "The Americans are in the game room."

He said, "Yes, and encamped upon the grounds. I do not want to . . ."

"Their mood is nasty and their patience is gone."

"I will be down in a moment. I must—"

Lavagni stepped in and said, "Ay, Monzoor. Where the hell you been?"

"At the hospital," he snapped. "An accident. I am not feeling well, Lavagni. Can we talk in the morning?"

"It's already morning," Lavagni declared. He could see that the Monzoor was not his usual suave self, but this was no time for tea and tears. "And we already lost four hours too many. We better talk right now. I got a message for you. From th' council." Lavagni spun about and returned along the passageway to the game room.

Roxanne whispered, "These men are extremely dangerous. I would recommend that we conclude our business and permit them to leave."

Rudolfi nodded gloomily and followed Lavagni toward the game room. Roxanne stopped him and helped him out of his overcoat. He groaned as the bandaged hand passed through the sleeve. She hissed, "What happened?"

"Bolan," he sighed, and went on.

Roxanne carried the coat and hat to a closet, neatly

put them away, then sank into a chair and lowered her face into her hands.

Lavagni was introducing "the boys" to their host. Rudolfi murmured a polite greeting and went to the bar. Lavagni said, "Accident, eh?"

He replied, "Yes," and filled a tumbler with bourbon.

The Washington *Caporegime* withdrew a notebook from his breast pocket. "That message, Monzoor. You prob'ly can't read my scratchings, so I'll read it to you. This is a directive, and it's straight from you know where. Thomas J. Rudolfi, Paris. Extend every co-operation and assistance to Anthony P. Lavagni and his touring party. Spare no expense and/or personal in-convenience toward assurance of a successful tour. Assure that all official and legal arrangements are both adequate and conducive to continued goodwill. Under-take no independent actions or activities which could conflict with the schedule for this tour. It's signed Better Trade Council. You'll get a copy by cablegram, so don't get no ideas of laughing it off."

Rudolfi sighed and sipped at the bourbon. "Why should I wish to laugh it off? Orders from the top are orders from the top. Of course we will provide every necessity for your tour, Anthony P. Lavagni."

"That burn on your forehead. It looks like some-body branded you."

"Perhaps."

"With a red hot barrel."

"How many members of your party?"

"Fifty-seven. We chartered a jet. We'll be going back the same way, same jet."

"When?"

"When the tour is completed. We expect to have fifty-*eight* goin' back. I gave all the stuff to Roxanne.

You see to it we don't have no problems at the airport when we decide to leave. Also I don't know that I dig those *Interpol* credentials. They look phony."

"The real article often does. I assure you that they are entirely genuine and will be respected by any policeman in France."

"Well awright but you better be damn sure. I ain't leaving no boys of mine in no bastille, Monzoor. It's a lot easier *keepin'* them out than it is *gettin'* them out. You remember that."

"Pray that you do not leave any in a *grave.*"

"You let me worry about that. What've you been doing to get yourself all bunged up like that? Arnie told you to lay off."

"Arnie does not command France," Rudolfi haughtily replied.

"The hell he don't. He's got a *seat,* remember that, and that seat says he commands."

"But that seat does not command the *lion,* eh?"

"*What* lion?"

"The lion called *Bolan.*"

Lavagni snickered. "Bolan ain't no lion. Except maybe around pussy cats."

Rudolfi's lips curled back in a sneer. "He has killed *twenty* good men this day, and *they* were not pussy cats!"

Quick Tony whistled softly and said, "*Twenty?* Last count I heard was seven or eight."

"It is now twenty."

"And one branded," Lavagni added solemnly. "Okay, you better tell me about it. No wait—that can wait. I wanta get the boys busy. They're goin' nuts." He swiveled about and whistled at the men at the billiard table. They straggled over to the bar, hard looking men who obviously were not easily excited.

Lavagni began issuing instructions. "Mario—your crew gets the airport personnel. Track down every one of 'em that was on duty when that plane came in last night. You know what to ask and how to handle it. Don't pass up anything, I mean not the littlest hint. We wanta know exactly what happened after that plane landed, right up until two hours afterward. Okay, Sammy—your crew takes the airline bunch, th' plane crew. I don't care where you have to go to find 'em—Rome or Timbuctu—you find 'em. Pilot, copilot, hostesses, the whole smear. You know what we want. Angelo, I want you—"

"I can save you all this trouble," Rudolfi interrupted.

"You ain't savin' us *nothing*," Lavagni growled. "We're startin' at the start and we're going through with a sieve. Angelo—your crew gets the cabbies, the subway people, the car rental places, airport buses, you know what. Don't overlook the littlest possibility. If somebody farted on a subway, you better know what it smelled like.

"Zinger and Littlefingers, you two divvy up the hotels. There's a lot of 'em, I know, but we gotta hit 'em all. Make it a quick skim, you can't spend too much time on each one or we'll be here a month. Start over on th' crummy side o' town, you know where, and fan through there solid.

"Now you all know what we're after, and I don't have to tell you again how Mr. Castiglione feels about this whole thing. He don't want Bolan's empty sack, he wants the guy hisself—so you know how to play it. You don't go jumping the guy, no matter how easy it looks, you don't go making no direct moves at *all*.

We all check in every hour on the hour, you know where I'll be. When we get a sniff, we don't wanta go chasing lost crews around. It's a big town and we wanta be in close touch. Now remember you play it cool. You spot the guy, you lay off and let me'n Wils go in and work the snatch. It's gonna be that simple, so there's no sense anybody gettin' hisself hurt or in law trouble.

"Monzoor has us all covered with the legal stuff, so don't get bashful neither. Throw your weight around on th' frogs if you need to, threaten 'em with arrest, anything you need to get cooperation—but listen—you all know this—we don't dare go home without this Bolan in our mitts. You know?"

The hardmen knew. They went out and gathered their crews into the bus and departed. Wilson Brown came inside, went to the bar, and carried a bottle to a couch and made himself comfortable.

Rudolfi sat in a thoughtful silence. Roxanne reappeared with dainty sandwiches and wine on a tray. Lavagni accepted a sandwich and waved away the wine. Rudolfi would not even look at the offering. Wilson Brown graciously accepted the entire tray and placed it on the floor beside him.

Presently Lavagni said, "Well Monzoor, I guess I better cut out. Mrs. Loureau knows where I'll be. I need a car."

"Take the Ferrari," Rudolfi muttered.

"Okay, thanks. Hey—don't be so down in the dumps. We'll get Bolan. And you'll get your cut."

"My *cut!*" Rudolfi sneered.

"Yeah. Lavagni was giving him a curious look. "What's eating you?"

"My *cut* is the *heart,* Lavagni."

"The heart of what?"

"The *heart* of the *lion!* I will cut it out of him myself!"

"Th' hell you will. You got the directive, Monzoor. I got six or seven witnesses to that. You better not go off on no cocky . . ." Lavagni left the warning uncompleted, nodded his head to the woman, and went to the couch to collect his companion.

Brown scooped up a handful of sandwiches, waved to the couple at the bar, and followed his boss outside.

As the Ferrari roared away, Rudolfi told Roxanne, "Tonight I met myself."

"What does this mean?" she asked, her eyes worried.

He brushed the half-finished glass of bourbon off the bar. It hit the tiles of the floor and smashed, the liquid spreading out in quivering streamers from the center of impact. "As that," he whispered. "Smashed—and everything inside spilling out."

"Are you all right? Your hand . . ."

"The hand will heal itself. The soul, never!"

"Let me help you," she whispered.

"No, I . . . well yes. There is a detail you may attend. Contact our friend, *M'sieur l'Androix.* Tell him the House of Celeste, on *Rue Galande.* All of the girls, all of them, plus the *madame,* I want them taken to Algiers."

"Thomas, *non!*"

"Yes. Tell l'Androix—they must go to the most devilish of markets, he will know. And tell him that he must find each of them—leave none unpunished. And tell him that I want this known, I want all to know."

"Thomas, this is—"

"This is justice, Roxanne. But for them, I would have bagged the lion tonight."

"But Thomas . . . *Algiers!* It is better that you simply have them killed!"

"That would not be enough. No. I want them taken to Algiers. I want them sold there, and I want them to know *why* they are being sold there, and I want them to contemplate their sins, and I want all of Paris to contemplate both the sins and the punishment. The example must be made. You will do this, Roxanne, without further question."

"Oui. Oui, Thomas. What else shall I do?"

"Nothing. I will do the rest. Let Lavagni's crew run with the sieve. Rudolfi has the aces."

The fear surfaced and spread across Roxanne's face. "Thomas, let them have him!"

"No. Rudolfi has the aces, and Rudolfi is even now playing a few of them. Rudolfi will bag the lion, Roxanne—or Rudolfi will die."

Roxanne was thinking that perhaps Rudolfi was already dead. This strange man with the wild eyes who would sell young girls on the *hideux* African slave markets and who defied the formidable powers of America—this man was not her Thomas. Where, she wondered, had he died?

A tired and troubled group of law officers were assembled in a small office in the Paris police headquarters. The ranking officer present, a slender young-old man with graying temples and quick eyes, tilted his chair back and slid a clipboard of reports to the center of the conference table. "We must conclude," he announced softly, "that Mack Bolan is in Paris. Stories concerning *L'Americaine Formidable* are being whispered throughout the Latin Quarter—and never since the days of the Algerian terrorists has such violence been done in a single day."

A young officer at the other side of the table quietly pointed out, "But there is nothing in the evidence, Inspector, to definitely establish that the man Bolan is this same *L'Americaine Formidable.*"

"Let us tabulate," replied the Inspector. "First, we receive a flash from the United States that the man known as *The Executioner* is suspected of having boarded Overseas Flight 721, Washington to Paris. At Orly, we encounter a man who meets every description of the one in question. But we are embarrassed. This American is identified as the film star, Gil Martin, beyond any doubt. We learn later that another American who fits the general description has been passed through with only a peremptory challenge."

"Yes, but this is merely—"

"Continue the tabulation with me, please. Less than one hour after the arrival of Flight 721 at Orly, a battle erupts in the *St. Michel* neighborhood. The victims are identified as known underworld figures, and the whispering is begun concerning *L'Americaine Formidable.* Approximately one hour after this, the same Gil Martin arrives at his hotel on *Champs d'Elysees.* Or—*is* this the same Gil Martin? If so, where has he been for these past two hours? Sightseeing in the fog? The doorman at the hotel insists that this man arrived on foot. He is surly with the desk clerk and orders a rental auto even before going to his room."

"But what are you—? Why are we back to Gil Martin, Inspector?"

"Let us see. Tabulate with me. Gil Martin goes to his suite and apparently to bed. Late in the afternoon he again appears. Again he is surly with the clerk, spurns an offer to speak with the most beautiful woman in all France, and departs in his rented auto.

"Now—let us jump ahead in the tabulation. At thirty minutes past the hour of ten, this same evening, another battle erupts in almost the precise same spot as the earlier one. This is *L'Americaine Formidable* with a vengeance. When our—" he gestured to a young officer at the end of the table, "—investigating team arrive on the scene, they find incredible carnage at the House of Celeste. The dead are scattered about all three levels of the house, two are lying in the street outside—but one, *one,* remains *alive.* This is none other than the esteemed M. Rudolfi, man of many involvements and influential connections—*but,* an American citizen—*American,* mind you."

"Surely you do not think Rudolfi is *L'Americaine Formidable!*"

"Wait awhile. Let us proceed with the tabulation. M. Rudolfi cannot explain what has happened. He was driving by. He saw what he thought to be a business acquaintance entering this questionable establishment. He goes inside, finds a madman killing everyone in sight, is himself wounded and left for dead.

"Now . . . to move back a bit in the tabulation." The Inspector's eyes went to a man down the table. "Would you repeat the events at Orly this evening, Claude?"

A heavyset detective removed a dead pipe from his mouth and reported, "A chartered jet landed at nine-forty, Washington to Paris. A large delegation of American businessmen were hurried through customs by some official prearrangement and were met by a special bus. These businessmen did not look like businessmen. The bus took them to a fashionable section near the *Arc de Triomphe*. There the bus awaited while three men went into the town house of M. Thomas Rudolfi—," his eyes flashed to the Inspector, "—man of many involvements and influential connections."

A man at the end of the table sighed loudly.

The heavyset one continued. "The bus was there until some time past ten o'clock. The passengers sat complacently, patiently, penned up in there, uncomplaining. At shortly before ten-thirty, the three men returned to the bus and the entourage proceeded to the chateau of M. Rudolfi. At last report, the bus remained at that location, as did all its occupants."

"Remember now," the Inspector reminded the conference, "that all items of the tabulation continually reflect American involvement. Rudolfi—we all know what he is and who he is. The American 'businessmen' —we know also who and what they are. The—"

The young officer across the way again interrupted. "Why do we not bring in this M. Rudolfi and put to him some cogent questions?"

The Inspector released a harsh sigh. "The impatience of youth. You will 'bring in' this man of many involvements only when you have resigned yourself to a premature retirement, or when you have caught him in an indefensible act of murder—preferably with 100 eyewitnesses and substantiating photographs. Now—let us again shuffle the tabulation." His eyes sought the young detective at the end of the table. "Petreau, you conducted the investigation at *Rue Galande*. Was there an American involved in this investigation?"

"Yes," came the soft reply. "I did not know at the time, Inspector . . ."

"I know, I know. Give us your item of tabulation, please."

"In the hotel directly across from the scene of the

crime, I questioned an American citizen as a possible eyewitness. I became convinced that he had no useful information." The detective sighed. "I left him in peace. He was in a . . . compromised situation . . . with a young woman."

"And you verified his identity, of course."

"I accepted the management's passport inspection. The manager identified the man I questioned as the same man who had checked into the hotel earlier that same day, at which time of course his passport was presented and registered."

"An American passport, I have noted."

"Yes."

The Inspector's gaze swept about the table. Obviously he enjoyed the dramatic. "And the name of this man, found directly across from the scene of the crime, this man who registered at the hotel under an American passport?"

"The name on the registry was Gill Martin."

"Yes, the name on the registry was Gil Martin. Could it not as well have been *L'Americaine Formidable*—or *Mack Bolan*—or *The Executioner?*"

The conference broke up shortly after that dramatic moment.

An item of reasonable proof had been established.

The Paris police had arrived at a logical course of action.

And a man who was then calling himself Gil Martin was moving into an area of jeopardy never before encountered during his young and savage career.

There was a uniqueness here—a quality of beauty which had nothing to do with the flawless skin, saucy eyes, and the raven sheen of contoured hair. He knew that he was looking at the most beautiful woman in his experience—but he would have been hard-put to describe that beauty to another.

Bolan was not absolutely certain as to just "oo" he should be. He dragged a chair over beside the bed and sat down.

The girl shrank back from his brooding gaze and said, "I demand to know 'oo you are."

He smiled suddenly and told her, "Since this is my room, and that is my bed, I think you should first tell me 'oo the 'ell *you* are."

She said, "Thees ees Gilbear Martin's suite."

Bolan nodded his head agreeably. "That's right. And I'm standing-in for him. So 'oo the 'ell is in my bed?"

She was peering at him with mounting perplexity. "Standing-een? But I do not—well, thees ees *crazy!*"

Bolan told her, "If you belonged to me, I'd spend about half my time just sitting and looking at you."

She moved head and shoulders in what he read as an unconsciously coquettish gesture and asked him, "And the othair time?"

Bolan chuckled. "Guess."

She remembered where she was, and demanded, "Well, where ees Gilbear?"

"Cooling it, relaxing. So don't you go lousing him up, eh."

"Do you know 'oo I am!"

"I don't care if you're Joan of Arc. Blow the whistle on Gil and you're a louse—a beautiful one, but still a louse."

"Blow the wheestle?" She laughed suddenly and cried, "Oh, *oui!* But this is delicious! Quickly now, 'and me my wrap and turn your 'ead."

Bolan did both. She moved out of the bed and into the flimsy garment in a single fluid movement, then leaned over and kissed him lightly on the cheek. "I am not the louse," she assured him. "Eeny-way, I am leave for Cannes een a few hours. I 'ave not the time for blow the wheestle. Tell Gilbear that Cici sends 'er love."

Bolan asked, "Ceci who?"

"Oh, *m'oui,* you are the lousy stand-een. You do not know of Cici Carceaux?" The girl was getting into a bulkier garment and fishing about with one foot for a pair of furry little bedroom slippers. She gave him a sharp gaze and told him, "Not eentirely lousy. The face ees strong, eet 'as character, more so than Gilbear. Cici could grow to love thees face, Meester Stand-een. Tell me, stand-een, what would you do weeth Cici othair than seet and look at 'er?"

Bolan chuckled and said, "I'd think of something."

She laughed again and said, "Well, eef I were not going to Cannes . . ."

"Isn't that on the Riviera?"

"Yes, eet ees on the Riviera."

"Close to Nice and Marseilles?"

"Nice, yes. Marseilles, not so close. Are you going there?"

Bolan grinned. "Someone suggested tonight that I may be happier there."

She was watching him through partially lowered lashes, the coquette resurfacing. "I do not like to drive alone. Come weeth me."

"You're driving?"

She made a wry face and told him, "Pairhaps you would do the driving?"

Bolan said, "Great. Let's leave right now."

"Agreed! Do you mind eef I stop by my suite and get some clothing?"

He grinned and shrugged his shoulders. "You look great to me just the way you are."

"Americains I love them!" she shrieked. "So eempulsive!" She ran to the door, turned back to him, and said, "Meet me een the lobby een feefteen meenutes."

"In the garage," he suggested.

"Oh-kay!"

The door closed and she was gone.

Bolan put a hand to his head and gazed about the room, wondering if she had actually been there.

He had never been in the presence of such an exciting, enchanting woman.

"Yes, she had been there. He could still smell the lingering traces of her.

Maybe, he was thinking, the game had changed. Maybe he would snatch a few golden moments from his jungle of death and discover what Eden was all about.

The Executioner should have known better.

Very shortly, he would.

11: Right On

Bolan took the elevator straight to the garage, again bypassing the lobby. He dropped his bags at the pickup station and told the attendant, *"Le voiture de Mlle. Carceaux."*

He was informed that the car was ready, and was directed to a gleaming Rolls waiting in the exit lane. The attendant turned over the keys and Bolan approached the car with sudden misgivings. He was stowing his gear in the luggage compartment when the woman arrived. She was almost quivering with excitement as she hurried over; a porter burdened with two large suitcases was laboring to keep up with her.

Bolan took her bags and stowed them himself. He noted that Cici was tipping the porter, then she opened a rear door and climbed in without a word to Bolan.

He secured the luggage compartment and went around to the driver's side, leaned in, deliberately measured the distance separating the front and rear seats with his eyes, and told her, "I didn't exactly have this in mind."

She said, "In the box—the compartment—what the 'ell you call—is chauffeur's 'at."

"You want me to wear a chauffeur's 'at?"

"Not that I want, but that I suggest. Also I suggest you should 'urry."

Something in her eyes told him not to argue. He slid into the seat and found the blue cap. It was a bit small but not hopelessly so. Bolan put it on, added his dark glasses, cranked the engine, and eased out of the garage.

They were stopped immediately at the curb just outside by a uniformed policeman. A quick glance right and left disclosed a swarm of them in the immediate area. Bolan's heart went into a tango and his mind shifted into survival mode. He had a hand on the door mechanism, waiting for the cop to step over to him, his thoughts racing ahead to the moment when he would make his move, catch the cop with a flying door, and try the breakaway on foot.

But the cop did not step over to Bolan. Cici Carceaux had her window down and was scooted to the edge of the seat, giving the guy a smile that would light two square blocks of Paris. The cop touched his cap and bent almost double in the sudden recognition. He murmured, *"Bonjour, Mlle.* Carceaux—*excusez-moi."* To Bolan he gave the slightest flicker of a glance and the command, *"Continuez."*

Bolan did so without delay, easing the big car onto the street and around to the boulevard. Police vehicles were all over the place and a dozen or more uniformed cops were on the walk in front of the hotel. He cruised on past, and not until the scene was completely lost in the rearview did he relax enough to ask his passenger, "Okay, which way to the Riviera?"

"Is this all you 'ave to say?"

He shrugged. "It's a sensible question—unless you want to end up in Brussels."

She was slithering over the backrest and moving beside him in a flash of well-filled nylons. "Follow the signs for Lyon," she directed breathlessly. Then she snatched the chauffer's cap from his head and removed the glasses. "Why do the police swarm all ovair for Gilbear?"

"Is that what that back there was about?"

"This you know! I encounter them in the lobby. They are confer with the desk and go up in great numbers to make the arrest. Uh-huh, it becomes more clearly to Cici, this masquerade. Gilbear is in great trouble, no?"

"No," Bolan responded, quite honestly. "It's all a misunderstanding. Gil isn't in trouble. Those cops, Cici. Any chance of them putting one and one together and coming up with you and me?"

She stared at him for a silent moment of confusion, then: "Oh, no. I do not think they even notice Cici, they are so occupied with othair things."

She settled daintily into the corner of the seat, against the door. Bolan could feel her eyes on him. Street traffic was practically non-existent, it being that dead period in Paris between the two worlds of night and day. They were moving swiftly along now, the powerful Rolls engine pulling them on effortlessly through the quiet streets.

He glanced at her, caught her direct gaze, and asked, "How far is Cannes?"

She replied, "Eight, ten hour, depending on the 'aste of the driver."

He whistled softly. "That's quite a drive."

"This is your fault, stand-in. I would 'ave been aboard *Train Bleu* and more than 'alfway to Cannes but for you."

Bolan said, "I'm sorry."

"You do not look sorry. You look most 'andsome and appealing. Anyway—I am not sorry. This is superior to the day train, an endless and boring journey. I say this for your benefit. The same train from Paris goes also to Marseille and Nice."

"Something wrong with French airlines?"

"For some, no. But for Cici, I will await angel's wings, not pursue them."

He grinned and told her, "You're pretty close right now. Uh, your accent is smoothing out. What became of the long *e*?"

She laughed and moved closer to him. "I am the natural fraud! Sometimes I do not know what is Cici and what is the cinema image."

"And what does that mean?"

"When I am cast in American films, I am told 'ow to accent the English. In Italian films, 'ow to accent the Italian. Even in French films, 'ow to speak the French. Sometimes I do not know what film I am speaking."

"Sounds confusing," Bolan muttered.

"Yes, it is confusion." She moved closer and her hand crept inside Bolan's arm.

He said, "Uh-uh."

"What this means, uh-uh?"

"It means you're tangling up my gun arm."

She giggled and pressed her head against his shoulder. "*M'oui,* thees ees threeling!"

Bolan experienced a deep irritation. He growled, "What film are you doing right now?"

She pulled away, sobering quickly. "I apologize, stand-in."

Quickly he said, "No, I'm the one that's wrong. I,

uh . . . thanks for getting me out of that mess back there."

Following a moment of silence, she told him, "I can speak the English better. I know 'ow."

He smiled. "You're still dropping your *h*'s."

She made a long face and replied, "The *h* is not a French sound. I will nevair do the *huuah*—it is like throwing out something that is not wanted. Language is the same as life, as love—it is a giving of something treasured, something of great value. I will not give it with the *huuah*."

Bolan sighed. She was telling him something while not actually saying it. A point of ethics. He said, "Okay, Cici, I'm the fraud. And you could be in great danger. I'm going to fade away when we reach the edge of town."

"No! I do not wish that you fade away!"

He glanced at her and said, "Look, this is no film, it's raw life. And you might find out just how raw it can get. I can't—"

"No!" She moved back onto his shoulder. "Take me to Cannes, stand-in. I have a villa—a 'ouse on the coast." She nuzzled his arm and added, "The raw life is there also."

Bolan could believe it. He silently debated the question, finding it more and more difficult to face what he knew to be the proper decision. He had no right to involve this woman in his difficulties, yet he could not find the strength of character to refuse her demands that he do so. They drove on in a continuing silence and suddenly they were whizzing along free and clear on the highway to Lyon and she was snuggled against him—the decision was lost by default—and Bolan was telling himself that he would get out at the next town.

At that next town he found that she was quietly sleeping, her soft and regular breath falling upon his neck just beneath the ear, and he went on through without slowing. The magic of her had its way and, by the time he made the first service stop, Bolan was telling himself that the danger lay behind them now, that there was no necessity for the noble sacrifice; and the golden moments of Eden were seeming more and more accessible and desirable and reasonable as a goal to pursue.

Cici awakened as he pulled into the service station, lightly brushed his throat with her lips, and got out to freshen herself.

Bolan stood by while the vehicle was being serviced, then he paid the attendant and went to the rest room. When he returned, a carton of soft drinks and a small bag of snacks were on the seat. Cici was in the telephone booth. She saw Bolan and immediately returned to the car. She said nothing, but began poking about in the bag of snacks. Bolan started the car and returned to the highway.

She opened a soft drink and handed it to him. "I was trying to call Paris," she told him.

He accepted the bottle and said, "Trying?"

"I did not get through."

Bolan accepted that without further question. She unwrapped a candy bar and gave it to him. "Turn on the next *Route Nationale* to your left. This will save us some time."

He nodded, slowed, and did as she suggested. Suddenly she surged over and kissed him lightly on the lips. He grinned and said, "What was that for?"

"For trusting me."

"Why shouldn't I trust you?"

She shrugged. "It is a world of distrust, is it not?"

He murmured, "Trust ends when doubt begins. Have you given me any reasons to doubt you, Cici?"

"No," she replied softly. "And 'ave you given Cici the reasons to betray you, stand-in?"

He chuckled and found himself relaxing. "I hope not, for both our sakes."

Bolan had not meant the remark as a threat. He realized, though, that it sounded like one. He felt her eyes on him but she said nothing. When he finished his drink she took the bottle from him and got onto her knees to place the carton and bag in the rear. Then she stayed that way and melted over against him, head on his shoulder, arms going about his neck. "Does this bothair your driving?" she whispered.

He replied, "Yes, but let it be bothered."

She laughed softly. "Do you truly have a gun?"

He said, "Yep," and unbuttoned his jacket.

Her fingers crawled down his chest and lightly caressed the pistol grip. "You do not break Cici's arm?" she asked, faintly mocking.

"Not yet," he replied.

"But when?"

He chuckled. "Don't put me on the spot, Cici."

She withdrew the hand and left it lying across his waist. Bolan drove on in silence. Some minutes later he decided that she was again sleeping. He used one arm to try to gently rearrange her on the seat. She clung to him. He sighed and merely held her clutched to him, and they went on that way until the outskirts of Lyon.

The sun was up and the city was coming alive. Bolan stopped again for service and the girl quietly disentangled herself. He asked her, "Have a nice nap?"

"I was not sleeping," she said. Her eyes flashed

playfully and she added, "You are vairy 'andsome when deep in thought, did you know this?"

He gently squeezed her arm and said, "You couldn't even see me."

"One sees with more than one's eyes, stand-in." She pushed herself away and out the door.

Bolan watched her enter another telephone booth, then he gave instructions to the station man and got out to stretch himself. She was still in the booth when he went to the rest room, and she was still there when he returned. He paid the bill and moved the car clear of the pumps.

When Cici finally returned to the car he casually asked, "Get through okay this time?"

She dropped a folded newspaper in the floor and replied, "Yes."

He put the car in motion and the trip was resumed. When they were clear of Lyon and again rolling free, she told him, "I also call Cannes. To 'ave the villa made ready."

Bolan had no comment to this. She pulled her legs beneath her and knelt on the seat, facing him. He glanced at her and smiled. "You make me self-conscious," he told her. "What are you looking at?"

She laughed lightly and said, "This was your idea. I, too, can sit and look, *cheri.*"

Bolan laughed, then silence descended for several minutes. Presently she said, "For many years I 'ave 'eard the rumors of young girls disappearing from the streets of France. Do these tales reach America?"

He replied, "Probably not. We have enough of our own disappearing. Why?"

"Why? Well, I jus' wondair if you believe them, such tales. It is said that girl-stealers keednap these girls and sell them in Africa. The white slave markets. Do you believe this?"

Bolan shrugged his shoulders. "I wouldn't disbelieve it. Lot of rotten things happen, Cici."

"Officially these rumors are disclaimed. Not one year ago such stories were discussed in the newspapairs and declared false. Jus' now, when I call Paris, I 'ear another of these stories. It sounds most diabolical."

Bolan did not comment. He wondered if she was simply making conversation. She seemed to be studying his face for reactions. She went on. "I am told that ten all at once 'ave been spirited away this time. A 'ouse full of girls, from the Latin Quarter. A 'ouse on *Rue Galande*."

She got her reaction. A muscle quivered in Bolan's jaw and he said, "That sounds like more film stuff, Cici. Where'd you get a story like that?"

"It is being repeated throughout Paris. It is said that gangstairs were killed at this 'ouse by a man called *L'Executioner*. These girls were thought to 'ave 'elped this man. As punishment, the gangstair boss is 'ave these girls stolen and sent on the underground trail to Algiers."

Bolan saw his Eden rapidly disappearing, flaring out like a shooting star in a black sky. His foot moved from the accelerator to the brake and the big car rolled to a smooth halt.

She asked, "What are you doing?"

"Turning around. I'll be leaving you at the Lyon airport."

"No! Paris is too dangerous for you now! And you could do nothing there!"

"I have to go back, Cici." He was thinking of a humiliated man with the mark of a pistol muzzle burned into his forehead. "I have to see a man on some urgent business."

"The man you seek is no longair in Paris," she declared quietly.

He shifted into reverse, then hesitated with his foot on the brake and asked her, "How do you know that?"

Even more quietly she said, "Would you believe me if I mention the name *Thomas Rudolfi?*"

The gearshift returned to neutral and Bolan glared at her, frozen frames of his mind flipping slowly into overlaying positions. He asked, "just what do you know about Rudolfi?"

They were halted on the shoulder of the road. The girl reached into the floor and picked up the newspaper she had brought from Lyon. She unfolded and refolded it and lay it across the steering wheel. The composite likeness of Bolan was there, blown up and occupying half of the front page beneath a heavy black headline: *L'EXECUTIONER EN PARIS?*

She whispered, "*L'Executioner* is in Paris no longer, is this not true?"

Bolan's face was frozen. He repeated, "What do you know about Rudolfi?"

"I 'ave known Rudolfi for a long time, stand-in. This is not the point. The point is that you cannot return to Paris, and also there is no reason to do so. You will find nothing there."

Bolan's mind was beginning to whirl. He snapped, "You seem to know much more than I do. So what are you suggesting?"

She showed him a wan smile and said, "On to Cannes, stand-in. You may plan your plans there, in safety. And perhaps you will be closair there to the problem."

He took her hand and squeezed it, hard. "Let's get it all on the table, Cici. I want the whole story, all of it."

"*Non*. Not now. But please trost me, Mack Bolan." She made the name sound like *Mawk Bo-lawn*. "And let me 'elp you."

He started the vehicle moving again, then his eyes flicked back to her and he said, "No go, Cici. Everybody I touch turns to ashes. I'm getting off at the next town."

"I weel not turn to ashes," she quietly assured him.

Bolan could almost believe it. He asked, coldly, "Who the hell are you, Cici? I mean, for real?"

"I am Cici Carceaux, for very real," she solemnly informed him. Her eyes moved in a somewhat muted echo of the coquette she had shown him back at the hotel. "Not many men in France would decline an invitation to Cici's villa."

An idea was beginning to form in Bolan's mind. Perhaps, he was thinking, the potential danger posed by this female enigma seated so demurely beside him would be a calculated risk worthy of challenging. Suddenly he said, "Okay. So long as you know the name of the game. You know who I am and what I have to do. If you'll risk me, then I'll risk you."

"On to Cannes, stand-in," she replied, smiling.

"Understand this," he added solemnly. "At this moment, we're even. We can say goodbye and, as far as I'm concerned, part as friends. But if we go on . . . and I discover that you are my enemy . . . well, you will be in very great danger, Cici."

"On to Cannes," she repeated, the smile remaining.

Bolan sighed inwardly and his foot grew heavy on the accelerator. Something, he knew, was screwy as hell about Cici Carceaux. At the moment she was playing the role of friend. He would accept that . . . for the moment. But he would watch her . . . and with his mind, not his heart. With ten female lives consigned to a living hell on his account, The Executioner could not afford a heart.

As for those moments in Eden . . . they seemed now lost forever.

12: *The Riviera Plan*

Most of the trip from Lyon to the coast was conducted in virtual silence and it was nearing noon when the Rolls entered Nice and eased along the main boulevard, *Avenue Jean-Medecin*. Bolan's thoughts had brought him here; now Cici's directions guided him to the specific objective he sought, the Mediterranean headquarters of an American press service.

He parked just off the *Promenade des Anglais*, the beach-front drive, and he and Cici went separate ways from there—she insisting upon performing a particularly important service for him.

Bolan first stopped at the telephone exchange and placed a call to the *Pension de St. Germain* in Paris. After some small delay, the breathless voice of Nancy Walker came pleasantly across the wire.

Bolan told her, "This is the alter-ego. Just checking. Are things all right there?"

She said, "Oh my gosh, they're turning this town upside down for you! Where are you calling from?"

"A safe place," he assured her.

"Well, burrow deep! Even *Interpol* is nosing around. They were here early this morning."

"There? At your hotel?"

"Yes. Real tough guys. Gill thinks they were phonies, but I don't know what—"

"Where is that telephone, Nancy?"

"This one? In the hall just outside my room."

"Could I possibly speak to Gil?"

"Well . . . I don't know . . . his poor hands. I'd have to hold the phone for him."

Bolan said, "I need to talk to him, Nancy."

"Just a sec."

After a short wait, Martin's voice announced, "You've blown the cover, boy. They're tearing Paris apart for old Gil Martin. What's more, your other buddies are hot on the scent. They were here this morning, posing as *Interpol* agents of all things."

Bolan asked, "Did they challenge you?"

"Hell no, I was under the bed. They were calling on Nancy."

"You didn't get a look at them, then."

"Only through the window, as they were leaving. But I'd bet my residuals they were Mafia. Where are you?"

Bolan told him, "I'm with Cici."

"Cici who?"

Bolan recalled uttering those precise same words a few hours earlier, and in just about the same tone of voice. He replied, "You're old loving buddy, Cici Carceaux. I picked her up in your hotel room."

"Good work, but I've never met the lady. We almost worked together once but the deal fell through at the last minute. Where'd you get the idea that—?"

Bolan said, "This is important as hell, Gil. No cute stuff . . . do you or do you not know Cici Carceaux?"

"Professionally, by reputation, that's all. She's currently the hottest thing on film, the sex darling of

Europe—but no, sorry to say, I do not know her personally."

"Okay." Bolan's voice was tinged with an I-knew-it sadness. "I guess that's all I wanted, Gil. Uh . . . you're right about that cover, it's blown all the way off. You may as well come out now if you'd like. But very carefully. Call the cops to you, don't go out on the street looking for them. They might shoot first and check identities later."

"Hell no, I'm staying put for awhile. Never had it so good."

Bolan could hear Nancy Walker's soft laughter in the background. He grinned into the mouthpiece and said, "Okay, see you in the movies," and hung up.

Yeah, Eden was a total flare-out.

He went back to the street and quickly to the press service headquarters. He stepped in off the street just as a guy was coming through the doorway from an inner office into a smallish room of quiet activity. A girl was bent over a teletype machine in the corner, another was busy at a typewriter at the far side of the room.

Bolan and the man stared at each other for a frozen moment, the guy doing a double-take on Bolan, then he stepped quickly back into the office and snapped, "Jesus Christ, get in here!"

Bolan followed the man into the private office and accepted a chair. The guy shut the door and went immediately to a filing cabinet, took out a bottle and two glasses, and told his guest, "I don't have any ice or mix, sorry."

Bolan said, "Thanks, I'd better have nothing at all."

The man promptly returned the bottle and closed the drawer, then paced nervously across the floor to his desk. Bolan told him, "Guess there's no need to introduce myself."

"Please don't," was the quick reply. "Just tell me why you're here."

"Are you Lon Wilson?"

The man shook his head. "I'm Dave Sharpe, bureau chief."

Bolan nodded. "I remember some feature stories from this part of the world. Two, maybe three months ago. An expose of Mafia connections, something about the drug traffic. I figure you know more than you reported."

"Lon did those. He's in Turkey now."

"You must have records, files, something. All I want is a list of names and addresses—people known to have Mafia connections in this area."

Sharpe smiled grimly. "Oh, is that all you want? Why do you think I had to send my man to Turkey?"

Bolan said, "I'm thinking of an *exchange* of information."

"What did you think you'd exchange?"

"My reasons for wanting the list."

"Huh?"

"I'll tell you why I want the names and what I intend to do with them . . . if you'll just give them to me."

Sharpe offered Bolan a cigarette, took one for himself, nervously exhaled a cloud of smoke, then said, "Any idiot knows why you want the names, friend. Also, any idiot who gave them to you would become an accessory to murder. Isn't that right?"

Bolan shrugged. "It isn't privileged information. Those names are a matter of public record, and you know it. If I could move about freely I could get them from various sources. But I can't move freely and I'm racing the clock. I need them right now."

"Why?"

"That's part of the deal. I can tell you this . . . the story will shake France."

"Yeah?"

Bolan grinned. "Yeah."

The guy was thinking about it. He said, "Convince me."

"It has to do with the ten girls snatched from a house of joy in Paris early this morning."

The newsman's hand trembled as he removed the cigarette from his lips. He said, "Then they really were snatched? For Africa?"

Bolan nodded. "I've confirmed it. And I intend to get them back."

"How?"

"That depends on you."

Sharpe seemed impaled on the horns of a moral dilemma. He stood in a silent cloud of smoke for a moment, then: "Over in that cabinet, third drawer, there's a file marked *LW*. I'm going to the john. Be back in about a minute. What you do while I'm gone is a matter of your own conscience, not mine."

Bolan smiled. "There isn't a police hotline from that john, is there?"

The bureau chief faintly returned the smile. "I'm not that big an idiot, friend."

He went out and Bolan went to the file cabinet. He found a small spiral notebook which seemed to fill his requirements and dropped it into a pocket. An oblong manila envelope contained small mug-shot photos with names pencilled on the back. This also went into Bolan's pocket.

When Sharpe returned, Bolan was standing at the window. He turned to show the man a tight smile and told him, "Well, I won't take any more of your time. On second thought I have everything I need. I'd appreciate it, though, if you'd put out a news story for me."

Sharpe gave him a wry grin. "An obituary preview?"

"You could call it that. The story, though, concerns the *why* much more than the *who*. Beginning very soon now, for every hour that those ten girls remain missing, a top Mafia connection is going to die."

A momentary silence, then: "Jesus Christ! So *that's* how . . ."

Bolan soberly nodded his head. "That's how. And I'd like to see the story go out. It's important that these guys know why they're dying."

"One every *hour?*"

"More or less. Until the girls are turned loose. And I suggest that somebody work out a method for verifying it when the girls are freed." Bolan stepped toward the door.

"Wait, dammit. How soon can I release this story?"

"Give me about two hours. After that, the sooner the better . . . and the louder the better. Uh, how about verification that the girls are free?"

"Can you keep check on the Nice TV station?"

Bolan said, "I'll make a point to." He smiled and departed.

There was nothing secret, of course, about the information in his pocket. The police knew those names, various agencies of the UN knew them, and they had appeared in syndicated news stories throughout the world at one time or another. Knowing was one thing; establishing legal proof was quite another; even in the face of legal proof, obtaining prosecution and convictions was often quite another thing also. Bolan did not need to establish legal proof, nor was he interested in political influence. Bolan merely needed to *know*. And now he did.

The rabbits would run for their holes, of course—if not right away, then as soon as the first one fell over dead. It would require all the skill of his trade to carry out the promise. Somehow, he would have to do so—and he would be required to run risks which he would prefer to avoid. But a lot was at stake. So, once again, he was finding himself faced with a do-or-die situation.

He was wondering at which side of the question he would finally find Cici Carceaux. Regardless of where she was placing herself, Bolan was resolved to use her as much as possible on the *do* side. She knew the country, she knew the people, and she seemed eager to help. Bolan was in no position to refuse any offer of help, no matter how suspect the source.

Cici was waiting for him in the car. In the back seat reposed a lengthy object in heavy brown wrapping paper. "Oh-kay, I found what you wanted," she reported. "In the Safari Shop. It is a formidable weapon. I could 'ardly carry it."

"Any problems?" he asked.

"For me, a citizen of France, no. Why do you need such a formidable weapon?"

"I'm going to be doing some big-game hunting," he replied quietly.

"The salesman assures me that this will drop the charging rhino," she said. "But there are no rhinos on the Riviera, stand-in."

Bolan said, "That reminds me. I was just talking to Gilbear. He doesn't remember you, Cici."

Very softly, she said, "Oh, my."

"You're not going to explain?"

"No."

"Okay. Point me to your 'ouse."

"Take the 'ighway to Cannes," she directed. "The villa is about 'alfway."

"I hope, for everybody's sake, it's not 'alfway to 'ell, Cici."

"Between 'eaven and 'ell exist many levels," she said in a small voice. "I 'ave not betrayed you, Mack Bolan, whatevair you may be thinking."

"Just don't betray yourself," he muttered. They were leaving the beautiful seaside city behind them and cruising along a beach drive lined with palm trees. He thought briefly of Miami and Palm Springs and many battlegrounds beyond and, for one flashing moment, knew an almost overpowering sorrow for himself.

The French Riviera would have made a nice setting for Eden.

He quickly flung Eden away once and for all and savagely discharged the destructive little flicker of self-pity. He opened his jacket and checked the side-leather with his fingertips. Cici was on her knees again, quietly watching him from the far corner of the seat. He stared straight ahead and solemnly told her, "I believe I was falling in love with you."

"And I with you," she replied, almost whispering.

"We make a nice pair of frauds."

"Yes, but I 'ave not betrayed you, Mack Bolan."

"Why did you bring me down here?"

"To save you."

"Oh, come on now. All this risk to save a total stranger?"

"I 'ave my reasons," she insisted. "And now, after these hours at your side, the reasons 'ave grown."

He sighed. "Cici, if there's a set waiting for me at that villa we're both going to die. I hope you realize that."

"What is this *set?*"

"Ambush, trap."

"There is no ambush at Cici's villa."

Bolan hoped not. He wanted to believe her, and not just for reasons of the heart. He needed a headquarters which would offer him easy access to the resort towns along the Riviera, a strike center which would put him within range of places like Monaco, Nice, Cannes, St. Tropez, Monte Carlo, Juan-les-Pins, St. Jean-Cap-Ferrat—the campgrounds of international high society and fellow-travelers. The villa, as described by Cici, seemed perfect for Bolan's plans, and worth the calculated risk involved.

"You are looking very angry," Cici whispered.

"I'm not angry, Cici."

But he was. He was thinking of another fraud, a refined Englishwoman masquerading as a whore—one who had sought the taste of life in purgatory and who was at this very moment probably descending into the hell of all hells. He was thinking also of a redheaded kid with plump breasts and painted nipples and of an entire line-up of faceless ones who had brushed past him with whispers of "merci." And an older one with bitterness in her face and spit at her lips for the pains of life. Yes, Bolan was angry. Very shortly now, that anger would be spilling out in the most coldly violent expression of his violent life and the most fearsome experience since the days of the Third Reich would descend upon this international playground—The Executioner in rampage.

13: Battle Order

The villa checked out clean and was in every respect ideal for Bolan's plans. The two-story archetype of Mediterranean architecture stood atop a low bluff overlooking a small private cove and beach. A lock-gate and extensive grounds to either side assured privacy. At the rear, winding stone steps descended from a marble patio to the beach and boat dock, where a sleek cruiser glistened in the Mediterranean sun.

At Bolan's suggestion, Cici sent away an old man and his daughter, caretaker and maid—and Bolan immediately went to work. He carried the package from the Safari Shop into the house and broke the big rifle down piece by piece, closely inspecting all critical components —then he oiled and reassembled it. It was a clip-fed Belgian model, accepting .444 high-velocity and sharp-impact steel-jacketed ammo, with a 20-power intense-field scope and range finder.

Bolan then took the rifle and a belt of ammo to the cove and sighted it in. Cici sat crosslegged just behind the firing line and watched with fingers in ears as he methodically test-fired the big piece at varying ranges, notating the required adjustments as he went.

This task required about twenty minutes. When it was done she asked him, "Is it a good gon?"

He smiled and replied, "Yes, Cici, it's a damn good gon." He showed her how to sight through the scope and explained the compensations required for drift and drop. She wanted to try a shot herself. He sternly lectured her regarding recoil-absorption, padded her shoulder with his jacket, strapped her into the rig, and allowed her to have at it from a stated position, per her own demand.

She squeezed off a single shot, missed target and bluff and everything else in view, and toppled onto her back from the recoil. Bolan chuckled and helped her to her feet. She was rubbing her shoulder and giving the rifle a dirty look. "I do not see why anywan would call thees damn theeng a good gon," she grumbled.

Bolan helped her out of the strap and bent to playfully kiss her offended shoulder. She caught his face with both hands and steered him to a nicer target and their mouths merged for the first time in a sweet-warm mingling of purest passions. She stepped quickly back, said, "There," and ran up the steps ahead of him.

Bolan muttered "Damn!" and followed her to the house. He disassembled the rifle and cleaned and oiled it while Cici made coffee and sandwiches. Her task was concluded ahead of his, and she sat in an almost embarassed silence and watched him put the pieces together again.

As they lunched, she told him, "Oh-kay, what is the plot? You 'ave murdair on the mind—'oo will be murdaired?"

"I'm going to get those girls back, Cici."

"But 'ow? With that formidable gon?"

He said, "Yes, that's how." He took the spiral notebook from his pocket and placed it on the table. "I have the structure here of the crime combine of Southern France. I've put out the word that one of these wheels is going to die every hour until those girls are returned."

She showed him a shocked look. "But this is the bluff, no?"

"Not hardly." He consulted the notebook, then dug in the envelope for a mug shot. He found the one he sought and threw it onto the table. "There's my first draft choice, Claude de Champs. Know him?"

She slowly nodded her head. "Vaguely. He is in the casino crowd. Yachting and that."

"That's just at the surface. He also handles about twenty million francs worth of illegal drugs every year, deals in contraband munitions, and is thought to rake about ten thousand francs a week off the top of various vice operations in Marseilles. What's the life of a society hood like this worth, Cici? Would you say it's worth one of those missing girls?"

"I will 'elp you," she quietly declared.

"I was hoping you would," he admitted. "But in a very limited way. Do you have maps of the Riviera? Good ones?"

"Yes. I 'ave survey maps, maritime maps, road maps. What do you wish?"

"I want you to help me locate these people. On the maps, though, just on the maps. I have their addresses."

She said, "The Riviera crowd is like one small community. I know most of these men." She was sifting through the photos. "I am ver' surprise at some, that they are in this collection. You are sure of your information?"

He said, "I'm sure."

"I 'ave the personal interest to 'elp you, Mack Bolan. I can 'elp in bettair ways than this. Cici knows Riviera like back of 'and. I will, at the ver' least, be your chauffeur."

"Nothing doing," he growled.

"Then I will 'ave to blow the wheestle."

He said, "I believe you're serious."

"Jus' try me for serious."

He gathered the photos and carried them to the floor. "Get the maps."

Cici jumped up and went out the door. Moments later she returned with a stack of maps. Bolan went through them carefully, selecting some and rejecting others, until he had the best representations of the coastal areas. Cici brought pencil and tape; Bolan cut and spliced until he had precisely what he wanted. Then he took a soft pencil and began a methodical cross-sectioning of the coastline from Monaco to Marseilles. In each section he taped a photo, three of them into St. Tropez, and ran triangulations from Cici's villa to surrounding areas. When he was finished he stood up and told her, "Okay, there's my battle order."

"I see nothing but confusion," she admitted.

"I can't afford to telegraph ahead to my next move," he explained. "What I mean is, I can't establish a track. I have to keep mixing it up, reversing ground, zigzagging." He looked at his watch, studying it. Presently he said, "We start with de Champs. If we can find him, I want to hit him at two o'clock sharp. The alternate target is Vicareau, right down the way here off the *Moyenne Corniche*. If I can hit either of them, I want to pop up next down here in Zone 4, below Nice. I'll hit Korvini there, or his alternate Bernard. Then double back to Monte Carlo and our syndicated gambling shill Hebert. Are you getting the picture?"

Her eyes were a bit sick. She said, "Yes, I get the peecture."

He went on relentlessly. "These are going to be daylight hits. That means you can see the blood as it explodes out of them. And it's not chocolate syrup or a trick bag of dye, it's the real stuff. They don't get up and have a coke with you when the shooting is over. Bits and pieces of them are missing and sometimes they flop about and yell and cry as they're going. I make it as clean as possible but sometimes . . ."

"I told you oh-kay, I 'ave the peecture."

"I let you handle that gun down there mainly so you could see the difference between make-believe and reality. Guns do more than look cool and make a commanding noise. They are very powerful weapons of death, and if you think the kick is hard from the butt end then you better hope you never get in the way of what's thundering out through the muzzle. The salesman wasn't kidding when he told you this piece would drop a charging rhino. The muzzle energy is close to two tons—nearly four thousand pounds of concentrated impact, Cici, and when those big .444's come tearing in, bone and muscle and everything else stands aside and lets it through. It doesn't make for pretty viewing."

Very quietly she said, "What are you trying to tell me?"

"I'm telling you that I am not under any circumstances taking you with me on a hit."

"Not even when I promise to blow the wheestle?" she asked meekly.

"Not even then. If you won't bug out, then at least resign yourself to staying put, right here, until I get back."

"I would theenk you would want me where you could see me."

"Why?"

She delicately shrugged her shoulders. "I 'ave been dishonest with you, no? I do not onderstand if you tell me now that you trost me."

He said, "Sometimes a guy just has to trust his instincts."

"You trost the instincts then, not Cici?"

He grinned. "Same thing, isn't it?"

She smiled back. "I guess so."

"Okay. Help me pinpoint these locations on the map. I need absolute accuracy, so don't let me down."

"I weel not lat you down."

Bolan hoped not. Together they put the finishing touches to the battle order, then he began gathering his equipment. "What's that other car in the garage?" he asked her.

"It is the American *Sting Ray.*"

"In good condition?"

"Yes. You will use it?"

"Uh-huh."

She asked, "What if the plan does not work? What if there is nothing any of these men can do to rescue these girls?"

"They'll find a way, once the message is in loud and clear." He looked at his watch. "Which reminds me, can you get the Nice television channel here?"

She nodded her head and went to the set and turned it on. "Why do you want the television?"

"It's about time for the story to break." He continued rounding up his things and asked her, "Do you have a pair of good binoculars?"

She replied, "Yes," and went to a closet, returning with a leather case.

"Put it with the stuff," he requested.

She giggled, a release of nervous excitement. "I thought you would look at the television with them."

Bolan laughed and said, "Cici, I want you to . . ." He let the instruction dangle and followed her intent gaze to the television screen and to himself. He was there in a huge video blowup, backdropping a man at a desk who was reading something in that polished tone used by newscasters everywhere. "What's he saying?" Bolan asked the girl.

She waited until the narration ended, then told Bolan, "It is the same as you have told me before. A high criminal will die each hour until the keednapped girls are returned. Thees man say that you are a bloodthirsty killaire, and that the police are determined to prevent you."

Bolan grinned and said, "Fine." He had the miscellany of equipment in his arms, the big gun slung at his shoulder, and was going out the door. He turned back to tell her, "If you want to help, keep watching that channel. I'm supposed to get word there when the girls are surrendered."

She ran out the door after him, hopped about nervously as he stowed the gear in the Sting Ray, then grabbed him in a wild embrace. He kissed her, gently pushed her away, and put himself in the car.

"There is a lamp on the gate," she told him. "If in daytime and the lamp is burn, or night time and the lamp is not burn—this is warning of dangair within. Oh-kay?"

"Oh-kay," he said, grinning. He cranked the engine

and spun onto the drive. Moments later he was out the gate and on his way.

First stop, just south of Monaco.

Target, Claude de Champs, society hood.

Weapon, Belgian Safari rhino-stomper.

Mission, squeeze the enemy.

Method, execution.

The Riviera War was on.

14: On Target

Wilson Brown came through the doorway with an awed look wreathing his broad face. "Man, did you hear what this Bolan cat is—?"

"Sure, sure I heard!" Lavagni growled. His hand rested on the telephone, as though commanding it to ring. "I already got most of the boys headed for the airport. Now if Sammy will just check in . . ."

Brown was not to be put down. "Well, that's just the grooviest thing I ever heard of," he declared. "Man, that Bolan cat is clear outta sight, he's—"

"He's stupid!" Lavagni said. "Leave it to a schnook to get all lathered up over a bunch of whores. We got 'im now, Wils, don't you worry about that."

"That's what makes it so groovy," the Negro persisted. "He must've known he was exposing his position. But that's just Bolan. Even over in 'Nam you could always depend on this cat to be the one draggin' in the sick kids and scared old women, even with a pack of Charlies chasing 'im. I think he actually liked those gooks. I remember one time—"

"Aw, shut up!" Lavagni yelled. "Don't gimme no hero stories about that bastard! Have you got yourself packed? We gotta be leavin' for Nice soon as Sammy checks in!"

"I'm packed, man," the black giant replied, his eyes dulling and seeming to recede into their sockets. He went back out the door, muttering to himself, ". . . but that don't say I'm ready."

In an earlier age, Claude de Champs would have looked most natural in a powdered wig and holding a jeweled snuff box, perhaps at the court of Louis XIV, or dancing gracefully in the royal ballroom while his less privileged countrymen quietly starved in the streets. This would-be aristocratic Frenchman actually claimed a lineage from The Man in the Iron Mask—a claim difficult to dispute since the identity of the man so grimly punished by the king of France was never historically established.

Claude de Champs insisted, however, that the man in the mask was a secret son of the crown and half-brother of the grand dauphin, and he often visited the fort at Ste. Marguerite, near Cannes, to stare sadly into the tiny cell where his purported ancestor was imprisoned for eleven years.

Copies of the iron mask were set into each side of the gates opening onto the de Champs seaside estate, and a massive coat of arms showing the mask beneath crossed swords dominated the ballroom of the castle-like villa.

The Man in the Iron Mask had never had it so good.

Nor would have Claude de Champs, except for his robber-baron approach to life. His first handle on personal wealth had presented itself during the German occupation in World War II, when the then young de Champs had discovered that collaboration with the enemy was far more practical and comfortable than resistance. Always the clever opportunist, de Champs had managed to greet the liberating Allied armies with a French underground rifle in his arms and a cache of looted art treasures to tide him through the post-war adjustments. This latter was parlayed into ever-increasing involvements with various illegal trade centers and, by the mid-fifties, de Champs was rather securely established in the higher levels of organized crime in France. As his personal fortunes increased, so also did his social ambitions. At the time that Mack Bolan was matriculating from high school to U.S. Army, Claude de Champs was travelling with the international jet set and had "discovered" his link with a glorious past.

Perhaps this accounts for the Frenchman's personal disdain for the Executioner's ultimatum. As he told his friend and close associate, Paul Vicareau, in the final telephone conversation of his misspent life, "There is no reason for worry, Paul. This is the American way, to make the noise and apply the pressure. It is an empty threat. This man has been in France—for what?—one day? Two? He is being pursued from quarter to quarter and does not dare show his face anywhere. How could he know of us? How could he hurt us?"

"Perhaps this is true," came the worried-cultured voice of Vicareau, a true socialite who had fallen onto hard times some years back, and thus into de Champs' area of influence. "Just the same, I would feel better if we could contact Rudolfi and have done with this mad adventure. Will you try once more to telephone him?"

"Certainly, Paul, I promise that I will continue until I reach him. The important thing is that we remain calm. Fear alone could be our undoing. To act frightened at this time is to confess guilt. Do you understand?"

Vicareau's sigh hissed across the connection and he replied, "Tell this to my wife, Claude. I regret the day that Viviane learned of my business involvements. She wishes to shutter the house and to hide in the cellar."

De Champs chuckled. "You would do better to regret the day that you took a wife, Paul. Even as beautiful a woman as Viviane—there are too many ripening apples on the tree, no? I will tell you what—when the madman has been apprehended and put away, you will come with me on my yacht to Capri. Eh? But two virile men, in the prime of their attractiveness, with six of the most beautiful young women from *Folies Bergere*. Eh? Does this not appeal to even the husband of Viviane?"

Vicareau tiredly replied, "Just find Rudolfi, Claude. I would not presume to argue with him as to his justification for this act—but his timing was extremely bad. Tell him to bring the women back."

"Be assured," de Champs murmured, and broke the connection.

He walked through his trophy room and a priceless collection of mementoes of his glorious ancestry, and stepped onto the balcony to survey his miniature kingdom. Could a common American hoodlum actually hope to challenge all this? These grounds were the showplace of the Riviera; the ballroom beneath him had entertained the royalty of Europe; his kitchens had pleased the delicate palates of the most prominent of international high society. De Champs was not quite so assured as he had seemed in his conversation with the panicky Vicareau. There existed, of course, a possibility of danger. But Vicareau and his whining . . . De Champs made a deprecatory sound deep in his throat and leaned against the railing to peer out onto the south grounds.

He smiled, remembering the conversation with the

bleating goat. No, de Champs would not shutter the windows and hide in the cellar, but . . . The Great Danes were prowling free within the inner fences. He would love to see the cocky American gunman try those fences; he would think that he had fallen into a pit of lions—as, indeed, the effect would be the same.

Just below was Pierre, the dog handler. Pierre, too, would love to see his pets exercised. De Champs called down to him, "The beasts look magnificent." He laughed and added, "They have the hungry look."

The handler was wearing a pistol in a holster at his waist. He touched the butt of the pistol with the back of his hand and called back, "I am not too sure of them myself, M'sieur. They strain for the hunt."

De Champs laughed again and raised his eyes to the south boundary of the Iron Mask Estate. A public road to the beach traversed that side of the property, fully five hundred meters from the house. A bright red automobile was stopped on the road and a barely visible human figure stood behind it. De Champs stepped into the trophy room for a pair of binoculars and promptly returned to the balcony and focussed the glasses on the vehicle. He called down, "Pierre, open the gate to the south field," and leaned forward over the railing for a tense binocular inspection.

The car was an American sports model . . . a tall man leaning across the roof with some object . . . de Champs sharpened the focus, caught his breath in a sharp gasp, and the signal to flee clanged into his brain one heart-stopping moment too late. The last image registered on the retinae of Claude de Champs' eyes was a fierce face leaning into the eyepiece of a big gunscope and a tiny puff of smoke erupting from the muzzle of a long firearm.

The hot chunk of steel-jacketed .444 closed the distance in something under three seconds, zipping in just beneath the binoculars and ripping through the soft flesh of de Champs' throat in a geysering explosion of blood and mutilated tissue.

The binoculars fell into the Courtyard of the Iron Mask and the man himself was flung backwards and through the French doors and onto the exquisite cherrywood of the Louis XIV era trophy room.

And so died another pretender to the underground throne of France.

Not even an iron mask could have saved him.

The Sting Ray was in traction and powering along the road even as the report from the big Safari model was still rolling across the fields. Bolan turned onto *Moyenne Corniche,* the fabulously beautiful coastal drive, and ran south to the nearest exit, then swung inland and began the encirclement of Nice, a small section of map lying across the steering wheel and guiding him. Twice he overshot dimly-marked backroads junctions and once had to ease his way through a small flock of sheep blocking the roadway, but he came out on the southwest edge of the city with five minutes to spare on his schedule, then headed directly for the chateau of Alex Korvini.

The photo on the dashboard showed a scowling man with hard eyes and heavy brows, a long corrugated forehead, square-jawed, grim-lipped. According to the Wilson data, Korvini had made it big from the misery of his countrymen in Italy in the grim days following World War II, hi-jacking American free aid materials and selling them at inflated black market prices to those who should have been receiving the life-giving goods without charge. Since then he had been involved in veritably every underground avenue of international thievery and trade, including drugs and the wholesale disposal of stolen goods, but his steadiest and most lucrative form of income had come from petty frauds and illicit business deals involving U.S. servicemen stationed in Europe and those of the U.S. Sixth Fleet in the Mediterranean. Korvini had been a French citizen since 1961, had never been arrested anywhere, and was regarded by his jet set friends as an astute international financier. Which, in fact, he was—with an almost unlimited backing of ill-gotten money.

Bolan scouted the country estate with quick passes on two sides, then found the piece of high ground best suited for his hard drop. It was about a quarter-mile distance and allowed excellent coverage of front and rear entrances, both to the property and to the house itself.

The chateau occupied a small knoll. Slightly behind, below, and toward Bolan stood a moderate-size barn. Through his glasses Bolan could see horse stalls, a small corral, an expensive American automobile parked in back, another in front of the chateau. A man in white dungarees and a blue denim packet stood at the front gate with a shotgun under his arm; another, similarly clad, guarded a small entrance at the rear of the property. Another pair of armed guards strolled about on the knoll on which sat the house.

Bolan continued the distant inspection, raising the binoculars to sweep the surrounding countryside. As he watched, two vehicles entered an intersection about a mile beyond the estate and proceeded up the lane toward the front gate. Cops!

He returned immediately to the scrutiny of the chateau. It must be soon or never. Windows heavily draped, upper levels shuttered. Some were learning. Suddenly the back door of the house opened and a stocky man ejected himself partially, said something to a nearby guard, and quickly went back inside. Bolan grinned, having caught a quick glimpse of shaggy brows and bumpy forehead as the man disappeared from view. Okay, he'd spotted the target—now to get him back into the open.

Bolan went to the Sting Ray, checked his weapon, and returned to the hard drop. The vision field of the scope was highly intense, reducing to about a five-inch real-diameter focus. He targeted-in first on the back door to the chateau, then tracked slowly across to the nearest guard on the knoll, read his range, corrected to six-inches above target, tracked back to the door, again ranged and corrected, selecting a door-hinge as the spot in his crosshairs.

He swung the track several times, practicing the route and getting the feel of the swing, then he settled into the piece, laying-in prone, and found his mark on the knoll.

The guard was lighting a cigarette, turned to directly face Bolan, legs spread wide, the butt of his rifle on the ground, muzzle-end leaning against his chest. Bolan was sighting on the stock of the grounded rifle. He gently squeezed off, hanging into the recoil to maintain visual reference with the target, held there to confirm the hit as the guard's rifle took the impact and transferred it to the man, and both fell over—then Bolan calmly tracked over to the mark on the door and was on the second target by the time the sound of the firing reached the chateau.

Korvini's contorted face suddenly loomed into the vision-field, mouth open, obviously yelling something. The crosshairs smoothly tracked upward to the six-inch fix above target—a mixture of conditioned instinct and finely-tuned reflexes sighed into the squeeze-off, and another item of hard persuasion was roaring along the two-second course.

Korvini's heavy brows fell into the eyesockets, the face collapsing in a grotesque reception of sizzling steel, exploding inwardly and spattering the backdropping doorjamb with skull fragments and jellied frothings of brain cells.

Bolan immediately raised off the scope and into the binoculars, sweeping the grounds for reaction to the hit. The object of his first round was kneeling on the ground and staring stupidly at his shattered gun. The other guard on Bolan's side of the knoll was moving jerkily between the first target and the second, obviously confused and shaken by the one-two punch from nowhere. Another man, racing around from the far side of the house, abruptly recoiled from the grisly sight at the doorstep and jerked about to yell something to someone not in view.

The man at the front fence was trying to conceal himself behind the gate post while pointing toward Bolan's hill. The police cars had arrived at that point and uniformed men were erupting from the vehicles and going to ground.

Bolan returned to his scope and calmly sent a round into the left-front tire of each vehicle, then repeated on the two cars at the chateau.

Another binocular scan revealed not a soul moving down there. Bolan went back to the Sting Ray, stowed the Safari, inscribed a small X on his map, and went from the chateau that misery had built.

The Executioner was on target. Monte Carlo was next.

15: The Judas Touch

Paul Vicareau's cultured voice crowded the long-distance connection, often swelling into a suggestion of mild hysteria as he told Roxanne Loureau, "Do not tell me that you cannot find him, Roxanne. You must find him and you must tell him to placate the maniac. This man is keeping his word! Do you understand? He is fulfilling this threat!"

Roxanne's voice was troubled and sympathetic as she murmured, "The police, Paul, surely they will stop him soon. Meanwhile I will certainly—"

"The police! They sit at maps and contemplate the strategy while the madman moves about at will. I do not believe the police wish to apprehend him! I believe they sit back and rub their hands and place the bets on who is next to die! What has happened to our organization? Where is the influence, the protection, which you and Rudolfi so glibly promise the organization?"

"Please, Paul . . . I am doing everything in my power. Do not believe that you are the only one who is upset. We are doing everything . . . believe me, everything. And please do not speak so plainly, the telephone is not invulnerable to—"

"Oh, oh, Roxanne—you do not understand the gravity of our situation! Listen to me! It has been very shortly more than three hours since this man makes his announcement. Already gone are de Champs, Korvini, and moments ago, Hebert. No one is safe, no *where* is safety, he moves about at will—have you heard yet about the attack on Hebert?"

Roxanne sighed. "No, Paul, I have not—"

"Then let this illustrate the gravity of our situation. Nowhere is safety. How does this man know where to go? What could be more secure than the casino at Monte Carlo? Hebert is there with a large party. Hundreds of tourists all about. Hebert has declared that he will remain in the casino until the madman is captured. He is called to the telephone. Four bodyguards accompany him. As he is standing at the table in the midst of friends a single shot rings out, a window above crashes, and Hebert is lying dead in the midst of friends. Now do you understand?"

Roxanne's voice was not overly steady as she told the troubled man, "I have understood from the beginning, Paul. Please believe that I am doing everything possible, but you too must understand—this is most difficult. I have issued the instructions—Rudolfi is not needed for this. Be assured, everything is being done to intercept the, uh, shipment in question—and the full power of the organization is moving to release you from this terrible pressure. In the meantime, you must exert every possible caution for your own safety."

"I am going to demand arrest!" Vicareau informed her. "I will ask the police to place me in protective custody!"

"They will demand from you an incriminating statement, Paul!"

"Better that, Roxanne, than to join de Champs, Korvini, and Hebert!"

"But wait! Wait another hour, Paul!"

"The next hour, Roxanne, could be Paul Vicareau's. No—I will wait thirty minutes. But I will never forget that in my hour of greatest need, Thomas Rudolfi is nowhere to be found. I will never forget or forgive this, Roxanne. Nor will any others."

"Strength, Paul," she murmured, "have strength," and broke the connection.

Things were falling apart, and she could feel the weight of the entire structure bearing upon her. Yes, Rudolfi, in this hour of greatest need, *where are you?* What wild plot of personal revenge has sent you scurrying to the south of France while your friends die about you? You and your *aces!*

"I will call Cici," she told herself aloud. "Yes, yes—I must call Cici at once."

The Executioner was sealed in. And all the time he'd thought he was doing it so cute! The tiny principality of Monaco had become a jug into which Bolan was tightly corked, the cork being represented by swarms of French cops at every road and trail leading out of the jug. Inside, in the bottle, things were not much better. The tourists, he thought, must be getting quite a treat. It would appear that the Prince was changing the guard at every street corner. Uniformed men were everywhere, stopping every one and demanding passports—and the entire area was buzzing with a carnival excitement.

For thirty minutes the Sting Ray cruised about seeking an exit, sniffing out roadblocks and turning back, and now Bolan had to admit that he had goofed. He pulled around in an inspection of the fabulous yacht basin, port o' call for certain Greek millionaires and international luminaries of every ilk, and found the same situation there; retreat by the sea was also cut off. He stopped at a public telephone and, after some delay, succeeded in getting a call through to Cannes.

The vivacious voice came on the line at the second ring, and Bolan told it, "This is the stand-in. *Comment ça va?*"

She replied in a rush of French.

He said, "You know I don't dig that. What's the action? Someone else there?"

She again replied in French.

"Okay, I get it," he told her. "You still watching television?"

She said, "Oh, *oui.*"

"Nothing of interest there for me yet?"

"Non."

His sigh carried audibly across the connection. "I had a hell of a time getting to Hebert. Now it looks like I walked right into it."

She asked a question, the only part of which he understood was, ". . . Monte Carlo?"

Bolan replied, "Yeah. And I'm sealed in. Guess I got too cute."

In a guarded and almost whispering voice, she told him, "Do not come 'ere, *Cheri.*"

He said, "The lamp is lit, eh?"

"No, I could not do even that. Listen, they are everywhere . . . on the 'ighway, inside the grounds . . . the eenspectaire jus' walk to the patio for confer . . . ohhh I have but a meenute and I would say so much. Stay where you are. Can you get to the yacht basin?"

"Are you under arrest, Cici?"

"No no, I tell them and I think they begin to believe,

I bring you to Nice, not knowing 'oo you are, and then you 'ave split from Cici, see. They are much eempress, I think, because the Rolls is 'ere and you are not. I ask you, can you reach the yacht basin?"

"I'm looking at it right now. Why?"

"When they leave, I will try to peeck you up in the cruisaire."

"Nothing doing. You stay put."

"But what will you do?"

"I guess I'll go to the most unlikely spot and sit my fanny down."

"What means this?"

"Never mind. Bye, Cici. It's been great." He hung up, stared at the telephone thoughtfully, then picked it up and placed a call to Nice.

A girl answered, the barest trace of a French accent in her English. "Let me speak to Dave Sharpe," he told her.

"May I tell him who is calling?" she requested.

"Tell him it's the man from La Mancha."

"Pardon me, sir, did you say La Mancha?"

"Yeah. Tell him I'm the used windmill salesman."

The girl giggled and said, "One minute please, sir."

The newsman's exasperated tones clicked on almost immediately. "This could only be one guy," he said heavily.

Bolan replied, "Right, the world's last living fool, but maybe not for long. I'm pinned down and digging a foxhole, maybe for the night. What's the feel from the other side?"

"Panic, sheer panic. You're a tough puncher, friend."

Bolan said, "Not tough enough, I guess. Listen, I have to make a tactical withdrawal. Care to handle another story?"

"It's how I earn my living," Sharpe said, sighing.

"Call it a cease fire, temporary type. It's a little past five o'clock right now. I'll give them until . . . say eight o'clock to produce the missing items. If nothing has developed by that time, I'm going into a full-scale blitz."

"That's interesting as hell, in view of the fact that you've already got the whole continent in uproar. Uh, haven't you been watching the telly?"

Bolan said, "Not constantly. I just spoke to my telly-watching service, though. I got no message."

"Well . . . maybe it hasn't gone out yet. But I was just talking to the station manager. They've had two calls from Paris and one from Marseilles, asking you to lay off until they have a chance to spring the merchandise. You didn't get that?"

Woodenly, Bolan replied, "No, I didn't get that. But change that story I just released. Instead, I'm accepting their assurances that the merchandise will be sprung . . . but only until eight o'clock . . . then, same story."

Sharp said, "For what it's worth, slugger, I admire your footwork. Just don't quote me on that."

Bolan chuckled. "Thanks for the immoral support. Maybe I'll see you around some day."

"I'll cover your trial maybe."

Bolan laughed and replied, "It will never come to that."

"Can I quote you?"

"Sure. I wouldn't live ten minutes after an arrest. You know that and every *Mafioso* in the world knows it. Penning me up would be an automatic death sentence. So I'll take it standing up, thanks, and in a place of my choosing."

"You talk as though you're expecting to get it."

"Well, sure. I may be a windmill-fighting fool, but I'm no idiot. It has to come sooner or later. I'm just banking on later, that's all."

The newsman sighed. "This had developed into quite an interview. Thanks, I appreciate it. But tell me this—do you expect to get out of Monaco?"

"I didn't tell you that I'm in Monaco."

"Didn't have to. The whole world knows it. At least, the French police are assuring one and all that you are, and that you'll never get out. They've got a little maginot line around the entire principality. How do *you* rate your chances?"

Bolan's mind was working furiously. "Didn't I tell you that I was blitzing at eight o'clock? Does that sound like I'm hopelessly contained?"

"Well, you did say . . ."

"I said a tactical withdrawal. You make out of that what you can. But don't give any aid and false comfort to the enemy. I'm blitzing at eight if they haven't produced, and they'd better understand that."

"Then you are *not* in Monaco."

"Hell I'm not saying where I'm not. Let the cops figure it out."

Bolan hung up, cutting off another question from the newsman. Then he returned to the car and got away from that immediate area. Several new items of thought were now bothering him. Uppermost, why the hell didn't Cici deliver that message? What kind of a damn two-headed game was she playing, anyway?

Secondly, why were cops so damn talkative? Didn't they realize that every hired gun the mob could command would be pouring into the tiny principality, an eight square mile area already jammed with tourists and fun-seekers?

Lastly, and perhaps most troubling, how could he deliver on his rash promise for the eight o'clock blitz? He was hoping that he would not have to deliver, that the wide publicity being given his grandstand play would filter into the underground trail, wherever and whatever it was, and that the girls would be turned over. But what if they were not? Could Bolan even *survive* until eight o'clock?

Well . . . he would give it one hell of a whirl. Where would be the most unlikely place in all of Monaco for Mack Bolan to turn up? Aside, of course, from the royal palace. Where else, but the fabled casino at Monte Carlo, where an execution had taken place less than an hour earlier?

Bolan checked his tie in the mirror, smoothed his hair, and made ready for the most scalp-tingling gamble of his career. He would lay it all on the line at Monte Carlo.

Six o'clock at Monte Carlo was like midnight at Vegas. The evening crowds were in the streets—ladies who could have come directly from Cardin or Dior, and men in formal wear, plus hordes of tourists in casual dress who seemed to be there mainly to gawk and exclaim—sidewalk cafes without standing room available—here and there a yachting hat and a dude in denims and deckshoes—and everywhere, on this particular evening, sharp-eyed detectives and uniformed policemen suspecting every male in sight of being Mack Bolan in disguise, until irrefutable identification proved otherwise.

Thanks to tightrope timing, Bolan himself was not challenged once during the hundred yards or so of his walk from the parked car to the casino entrance. Just outside the door stood a congregation of uniformed cops. Bolan passed right through them and received his first challenge inside, by two gracious men in formal wear. It was a routine thing, the showing of passports to gain admittance.

Bolan was prepared for this, also. He opened his coat wide to get to the wallet, allowing his sideleather and hardware to come into plain view, then flashed the folder rapidly past their eyes, which were already distracted by the sidearm display, and said, "Police."

He was passed right through and not even required to pay the five franc entrance fee.

Inside the big gaming room was business as usual. Bolan found the spot where his latest target had gone down. The window across the way had already been replaced and the mess at the telephone desk cleaned up. A small throw-rug now covered the carpeting on the spot where Hebert had stood—to conceal the blood-stains, Bolan surmised. He casually made an inside inspection of the angle for that hit and realized that it had been a mighty tight one. Six inches one way or the other and it would have been impossible. *Something* seemed to be on his side.

He kept moving, pausing here and there to drop a few francs at a roulette table or card game, trusting his instincts to spot the plainclothes cops and to keep his distance from them. At a little after seven o'clock he went back through the lobby and into the admission-free room of slot machines. Here the traffic was thicker and the clientele more casually dressed. He pushed through snatches of conversations in a myriad of languages, found an open machine, and began unhurriedly feeding it.

At about twenty minutes past seven, he went to the cashier's desk for more coins. As he was moving away, a large black man stepped up to the counter and grinned at him. Bolan's brain clanged and seized on an instant recognition. His eyes kept the secret, he returned the smile, and he went back to the slot machine.

A moment later the big guy was standing beside him, feeding a coin into the next machine. The familiar basso voice advised him, "Just keep looking straight on ahead, Sarge, you're being scouted."

Without turning his head, Bolan said, "You're a sight for homesick eyes, Lieutenant. Who's scouting me?"

"Some guys." The black man fed in another coin and pulled the handle. "You're in a hell of a spot, aren't you?"

"Yeah. Did you bring me a crying towel?"

"No, I just brought myself. This is weird, Sarge. It's your voice, it's *you,* but it's the wrong face."

"How'd you spot me then, Lieutenant?"

"You kidding? Kids outside are already selling souvenir pictures of you."

Bolan grunted and watched the combination come up on his machine. "You're a long way from home . . . football season and all."

The Negro made a small payoff hit, chuckled gleefully, and scooped the coins into a huge paw. "My football days are gone forever, Sarge. Claymore mine, 'bout two months after we parted company at Song Lai. I been wearing a synthetic foot for about a year now."

Bolan said, "Damn! That's tough!"

"Don't give me no pity. I already gave myself all of that I can stomach."

"Guys do that."

"Yeah. I even forgot who I am, I guess. I just been another nigger for a long time now."

Bolan said, "You never were a nigger, Lieutenant."

Brown played with the coins in his hand and swiveled about to peer toward the head of the room. He sighed. "I been watching your maneuvers, Sarge. I been remembering what it was I used to like about you."

"We always worked good together, Lieutenant."

"Yeah. I'm over here with a Mafia crew, let's get that out right now."

Bolan's hand jerked to the slot and he dropped in another coin. Through a suddenly constricted throat, he said, "Yeah?"

"Yeah. I'm supposed to be luring you outside for a quick and quiet snatch."

"I'd prefer a sudden, loud bullet, Lieutenant."

"Well, see, that ain't the game. The game is, get Bolan alive. This cat back in Virginia wants to pit-barbecue you, I think."

"What's *your* angle?" Bolan muttered.

"A hundred grand does a lot of persuading, Sarge."

"So why the tip-off?"

"Like I said, I been remembering what I liked about you. I got to realizing you're a soul-brother, man. I decided soul-power is better than green-power any day."

Bolan felt himself relaxing, his blood thawing. He fed the slot with a mechanical movement and asked, "So what now?"

"You might have noticed, they got a police problem in this town."

Bolan chuckled. "Yeah, I noticed."

"Our crew boss is a guy named Lavagni. Know him?"

"I've heard of him. What's he look like?"

"Little guy, thick built, mean eyes. He's standin'

back there in the lobby right now, wondering what I'm doing all this time. Pretty soon he's gonna get nervous and come looking."

Bolan said, "You're the Lieutenant. How do you read the play?"

"Like I said, they got a police problem here. So much of a problem that Lavagni conned the local fuzz into giving his 'Interpol' crew a territory. He's got fifty men out there, Sarge."

Bolan whistled softly. "Sounds like quite a set."

"Yeah, and cute too. We got the central access to the boat harbor."

"You talking about the yacht basin?"

"That's right. And we got a yacht down there. That's how he's figuring to get you out past the cops."

Bolan was thinking about it. After a brief silence, he told Brown, "Then maybe that's my out. How are you supposed to be working this set?"

"I'm supposed to be telling you I got a boat down there. You're expected to flip with gratitude and run right down there with me."

A wary little signal ticked up in Bolan's brain. He said, "Isn't that exactly what you're telling me, Lieutenant? And haven't I already sprung for the bait?"

Brown laughed softly. "Sounds like it. Look you do what you like. I don't blame you for being suspicious. But I *am* leveling with you."

Bolan was torn across the decision. He looked at his watch, saw that it was nearing seven-thirty, and slid into the only decision available. "How many men on the boat, Lieutenant?"

"Five, at last count. Plus a guy and his wife, owners. They're in it, too, by the way. Some contact Lavagni made at the last minute, local types. The boat ain't the problem. The problem is those last fifty feet of pier before you get to the boat. It's a hard set, and they're supposed to take you without firing a shot, right there, then hustle you onto the boat. Then a fast run down to Nice, that's only about ten miles I guess. From there to the airport and then it's bye-bye birdie, straight to Dulles."

Bolan grunted and fed another coin into the slot machine, pulled the handle, and scored. He listened to the shower of coins and muttered, "Could that be a symbol of something?"

Brown laughed drily. "Don't count the winnings, man. If it turned out to be thirty pieces of silver I'd shit a klinker."

Bolan left the coins in the tray and asked, "What are my chances of blasting through that last fifty feet?"

The big man shrugged the running-back shoulders. "I'd say pretty squeaky. Orders are to take you alive, but you know what'd happen if you started unloading."

Bolan grimaced. "Yeah," he growled. "Well . . . okay, how's it supposed to go?"

Brown released a heavy sigh. "We're supposed to walk out of here like long-lost brothers and head for the harbor. Lavagni's troops will be running interference, keeping the real cops away. He's watching right now, by the way, so you gotta let me recognize you first."

Bolan spun about and looked directly at the big man for the first time during the conversation. A tight smile gripping his face, and in a voice of subdued excitement, he declared, "I'll be damn! It's Lieutenant Brown, isn't it? Hey, I almost didn't recognize you in those dude clothes!"

The black man stared at him closely, Bolan leaned

toward him and whispered something, the black face altered rapidly from a thoughtful frown to a happy grin, and their hands came together in a tight clasp. When they walked away together some moments later, the silver coins from Bolan's score still lay in the slot-machine payoff tray.

Perhaps there were thirty pieces of silver there; perhaps not.

No one had bothered to count.

16: And Then There Were None

The two men passed through the crowds and out of the casino, walked casually and without challenge to Bolan's vehicle, and paused there while Bolan leaned inside, looped a nylon cord over his head and tucked something beneath his coat in a quick motion that would have been difficult to detect, in the darkness, from even a few feet away.

As they walked on toward the harbor, Wilson Brown asked his companion, "That a stutter-gun you got there?"

Bolan said, "Yes. Thirty-round clip and two spares. You better hit the water when I say *hup* and I mean without delay."

Brown commented, "A sweep up the middle, huh?"

"That's right. One-man style. Is that Lavagni skulking around back there to the rear?"

"That's him. Also Sammy Shiv and crew. That means . . . let's see—about five on the boat, ten or twelve behind us—you know what you're walking into, man?"

"I know what I'm walking out of," Bolan replied.

"You better know what you're walking into, too. Right about forty guns posted along the end of that pier. Some are on boats tied alongside, and I think they even got some sittin' out in the water, in little boats. You got an extra gun?"

Bolan said, "You want it?"

"Yeah, Lavagni won't let me pack." He chuckled. "Thinks I'm a greenhorn, I guess."

Bolan laughed lightly and slipped the .32 out of the sideleather and into Brown's big hand. "There's a live one right under the hammer," he warned. "Six rounds are all you've got, Lieutenant."

"I can remember a time when we had less than that between us."

Bolan's voice came back softly solemn. "You've joined a loser, you know. These guys are never going to forget this. *Or* forgive it."

"I was born losing, man. Don't worry 'bout me. These guys ain't never going to know what side I was on here."

"You know how I feel, Lieutenant."

"Sure. Don't mention it." He chuckled. "What's a hundred grand mean to the soul? Can't take it with you, man. Can't even buy you no new feet."

"You're walking great," Bolan told him.

"Sure, I can even run. But not with a football, I mean not straight at the monster men. All the money in the world can't buy that back." He sighed. "Guess that's all I ever really wanted. Can't buy it now, man."

"You been making a good living?" Bolan inquired. The pier was in sight now, and he was beginning to tense-up inside.

"Naw, I been stealing one. Rehab center found out I was a natural for figures, made me a bookkeeper. Desk job, you know. I juggle books for Lavagni, the numbers game."

Bolan said, "No kidding." They were on the pier and

moving swiftly along. The main group to the rear was holding at the entrance, two or three drifting on in casual pursuit.

"Yeah, no kidding. Most of what I picked up at Cal was football, you know. I mean, face it, I *majored* in football, man. Then I majored in *war*. Then I majored in *disability,* and then *crime*. Yeah. Wils Brown was born at *zero* and has been steadily descending ever since."

"Don't say that."

"Yeah I'm saying that. You know I guess what I dig about you, man, is your *guts*. You know you've got a weird combination there, Sarge—tough guts and warm heart. Most cats don't know how to carry both."

"It seems that *you* do," Bolan murmured.

The Negro laughed. The .32 was all but hidden in the big hand. He said, "Well maybe you made me look at myself again, Sarge. You did it once before, in 'Nam—remember? Hey you better get set. There's a drop to your left, the sailboat. Watch that cat standing down in the cabin. The big boat ahead, with all the lights, that's where we're headed. The *Viviane.*" He chuckled tightly. "That's French for *last chance to live*. You better make it work."

They had slowed their pace. Bolan asked, "Where do they make their move?"

"About twenty steps ahead. There's suddenly gonna be about ten guys standing there, then there's gonna be 'bout ten right behind you, and you're suddenly gonna be in a crowd."

"This is another Dak Tung," Bolan snapped.

"That's what it is."

Bolan muttered, "Thanks, Lieutenant," and threw a sudden lunging block into the big guy, sending him crashing through the railing and into the water. The same motion carried Bolan onto the stern of a glistening pleasure cruiser. Thirty feet or so ahead, at the bow of the same boat, a group of men who had been in the process of moving onto the pier were now frozen and staring toward Bolan in obvious confusion over the surprise move.

Bolan's *pistolet* wiped away the confusion in a chattering message that sent men sprawling about the pier and the deck of the boat as he charged the group, firing on the run. Answering fire came from behind him as he leapt back onto the pier, projectiles thwacking into the side of the boat and chewing up wood about his feet. A searchlight came on back there and lasted through one squeeze of the Executioner's trigger finger.

An excited voice was commanding, "Wing 'im, dammit just wing 'im, aim for the legs!"

Fire was coming in from all sides now. Bolan took a grazing hit on the left arm and another furrowed his thigh. He went down and pulled himself behind a mooring spool, jammed a fresh clip into the machine-pistol, and sent a searching pattern of fire toward the rear and the voice of command which was still demanding that Bolan be taken alive.

His search scored and the voice ended in mid-screech, and another one reported, "Goddammit, he got Tony!"

The same voice then cried out, "Hold your fire, hold it! Everybody back here, 'cept you boys on the Viviane! Wait 'im out, I think he's hit!"

Bolan was not waiting for anybody. Already he was wriggling along the pier, keeping to the shadows of the big yacht, *Viviane,* listening to the rustlings and scurrying sounds of the enemy regrouping into their holding position.

Another searchlight came on from a boat downrange and began sweeping the area Bolan had just vacated.

At the far end of the pier another movement was beginning, as police began hurrying toward the sounds of warfare.

Someone behind him announced, "Cops are coming! How much longer can we wait, Sammy?"

Bolan had reached a point where the main deck of the yacht was level with the pier. To this moment, the firefight was barely a minute old. He could not give them time to regroup their senses, as well. He rolled swiftly onto the deck of the yacht, fell lightly into a deeper shadow, and pulled himself up in a test of the wounded leg. It held him okay, but the blood was oozing out and soaking his pantsleg. The arm wound burned like hell but was apparently bleeding very little and already clotting. He pressed the fabric of his clothing into it to help the process and moved quietly along the shadows of the deck.

Brown had said *five guns* aboard the yacht. If he could catch them bunched up, he just might . . .

Only the cabin lights were on now. Someone was cranking the engine. It caught, and rumbled into a soft purr. A voice from somewhere up above called out, "Hold it, just hold it, don't get nervous."

Bolan moved quietly to the outboard side and found himself peering through an open cabin window onto a handsome couple, a smooth-looking man of about fifty, a beautiful platinum blonde woman of maybe forty, both of them cringing low in the pilot chairs. The *pistolet* muzzle edged into the opening and Bolan softly commanded, "Do not make one sound."

The man's hands went up and he declared in a quavering whisper, "M'sieur, I am not armed."

The woman's eyes were haunted holes of terror. Her lips were forming words that would not come, and Bolan was hating these lousy wars more than ever.

He had recognized the man instantly, from a photograph on his battle order. He said, "Okay, Vicareau, who else is aboard?"

"Four men, M'sieur." The man's eyes rolled toward the overhead. "Upon the flying bridge, all of them."

"Okay, tell the lady to relax," Bolan whispered. "Maybe you've bought yourself something. Get this thing moving, high gear."

"Impossible," the man hissed. "The mooring lines, M'sieur."

"Never mind that. Just throw the power to it, all you've got."

The man swallowed hard and his hand moved to a control. Seconds later the deck was quivering beneath Bolan's feet and the entire craft was vibrating in the strain to free itself from confinement.

A muttered curse drifted down from above and the sound of moving feet directly overhead sent Bolan spinning into the open. The four guns were crowding the rail of the flying bridge in an attempt to determine what was happening below. They saw Bolan at about the same instant, but he was readier, and he zipped them in a blazing criss-cross and they went down like wheat before a scythe.

Bolan allowed the *pistolet* to hang free and grabbed a fire-axe from the cabin bulkhead and moved swiftly to the bow. A voice down the pier was yelling hoarsely as he hacked the line free. The bow immediately swung outboard and another hail of fire came in as Bolan hurried along the shadows toward the stern.

There was a mixture of gunfire now, from far back; Bolan supposed that someone had opened fire on the police, and now a full scale battle was raging back there. He chanced a run to the open stern and delivered a smashing chop to the tautly quivering line. It parted halfway through, twanged into a rapid unravelling, and then gave altogether with a loud pop—and the *Viviane* was loose and surging away from the pier.

Two men ran into the open on the pier, blazing away at Bolan in a rapid discharge of weapons. His *pistolet* swung up from his side in a quick retort, the two went down, and Bolan dragged himself back along the deck toward the cabin, his thigh gushing blood again and the arm burning from the exertion with the axe.

Viviane was about fifty yards clear now and throttling back for better control into the channel, and up ahead two fast police cruisers with searchlights were whizzing toward the fleeing yacht, with a rapid interception already a foregone conclusion.

Then like out of a pleasant dream Bolan heard the hot-honey voice of Cici Carceaux calling, "Stand-een, stand-een!"

She was pulling alongside in the sleek little cruiser which Bolan had last seen snuggled into the boat dock at the Cannes villa. As naturally as though he had been rehearsing the scene for years, Bolan climbed the rail and dropped into the cockpit of the cruiser. She went on around in a wide, power-off circle, swinging close to the pier as the yacht charged on into the channel—and as she idled about, Bolan noticed a floating figure in the water not ten feet away, a dark face turned toward the sky and white teeth gleaming in the moonlight in the most tranquil expression Bolan had ever observed on that big beautiful black face.

He touched Cici in a holding signal and leaned over the gun'l to hiss, "Lieutenant—come on aboard!"

"Go on, man," came the quiet reply. "Don't go messin' me up now."

Bolan gave him a grin and a restrained wave, and Cici notched the powerful engine into a quietly murmuring advance. She hadn't been kidding; she knew the area like the back of her 'and, evidenced by a skillful navigation in and around and through the orderly rows of anchored craft—and when they reached open sea they were quite alone and unpursued and roaring free.

Bolan took the wheel then and Cici took over with the first-aid kit. "Oh-kay, drop the pants, stand-in," she commanded.

"Hell, I thought you'd never ask," he told her.

It was nearing nine o'clock when they reached the sheltered cove between Nice and Cannes. Bolan's wounds were clean and bound up and adjudged negligible, and Cici had also cleared up a couple of points which were bothering Bolan's mind.

The police, she explained, had been at the villa since shortly after Bolan's departure and had remained until just past Bolan's telephone call from Monaco. They had connected her with Bolan because of the message she had left for Gil Martin at the hotel in Paris, and had strongly suspected a continuing association due to her abrupt departure from that same hotel—and at about the same time as the police close-in there. They had quit the stake-out, with apologies, and presumably gone on to Monaco to bolster the forces there.

Her eyes dancing with the excitement of the adventure, she added, "They should 'ave known bettair, no? To leave Cici free to dart to the scene in 'er cruisaire and loosen the jaws of this trap?"

Bolan found himself entirely reluctant to question her further, but he did ask her about the message-failure regarding the requested cease-fire.

"But it did not come ovaire," she explained, "until the vairy moment that you 'ang up the telephone."

Bolan left things right there and they huddled together in a silent run for the balance of the trip. They tied up the boat and went arm-in-arm up the stone steps, Cici crutching him a bit as he favored the injured leg.

Then went into the villa and she undressed him as he stared grimly at a French television play. Then she rechecked both wounds, cleaned them again and applied fresh dressings, and tried to put him to bed.

He dropped into a chair instead and told her, "Hell I'm not through. If something doesn't come across that tube for me pretty soon I'm going back out."

Cici clucked furiously and threw a blanket over his chair, then went into the kitchen to prepare "a queeck peeck-you-up."

Bolan grinned and left the chair momentarily to retrieve his machine-pistol, inserted his final clip of ammo, sat back down with the weapon in his lap, pulled the blanket over him, and continued his grim watch at the TV set.

A few minutes later Cici delivered a tall glass of mixed vegetable juices, with "jus' a leetle brandy" blended in. It tasted terrible but Bolan dutifully addressed it and had it half gone when the TV play suddenly blanked off the screen and a dramatic voice began an unscheduled announcement.

Bolan caught the words "L'Executioner" and "Bolawn." He sat up alertly and snapped, "What is it, Cici?"

In a hushed voice, she said, "A moment."

Then a picture came on, not very good quality and badly-lighted, but one of the nicest pieces of film Bolan had ever viewed. It was an interior scene, probably a police station, and a group of women were emerging from a passageway and entering a large room. Judy Jones was there, and Madame Celeste, and eight other weeping young women—Bolan counting closely. They looked like they'd been to hell and back, he decided, and probably they had, but thank God they were all there and proceeding under their own steam.

Bolan found his own eyes misting over and he quietly commented, "Oh hell that's great. Where is this, Cici?"

"Marseilles," she told him. "The police station near the waterfront. The announceire says an anonymous telephone call directed the police to an eempty ware-'ouse near the 'arbor. And 'e says they are all well and thankful to be free. They are to be 'ospitalized, jus' the same, for obsairvation." She turned to Bolan with glowing eyes and added, "This is wondairful, this thing you 'ave done—no mattair 'ow many rats you 'ad to keel to do it."

The weight of the day was now showing in Bolan's face. With success came also the inevitable letdown, the slowdown of vital juices, the cessation of stubborn determination to push on whatever the price.

Cici went to the TV set and switched it off, then

turned to him with compassionate concern. "You mus' go to bed now," she told him. "It is done."

It was not, however, quite done. As Cici was crossing the room toward Bolan, the front door opened and a wild looking man stepped into the house. He had a big fancied-up luger in his hand and a circular burn on his forehead and he announced triumphantly, "So I have snared our lion."

Bolan stared at the man through his weariness, and only vaguely heard Cici's cry of, "Rudolfi, no!"

Bolan said, "Get out of here, Cici." He tossed off the balance of the drink she had made him and threw her the empty glass. "Fix me another one of those."

"Yes, a last drink would be most fitting," Rudolfi agreed. "Fix him another of those, Cici, but do not make it too large—he will not have time to finish it." His pleasure obviously knew no bounds as he told Bolan, "Well, would you not wish to bargain again, M'sieur Executioner? I have sat out there in the darkness awaiting you for many hours, thinking of the many deals we could make. But you sneak in from the sea, eh? I did not consider this—but just as well, the wait makes the banquet sweeter, eh? Tell me, Bolan—what do you offer in exchange for your life, eh?"

Tiredly, Bolan said, "It's okay, Cici, he just wants to talk. Go on and fix me that drink. I mean it, go on."

Something in his eyes cinched the argument. She went hesitantly to the kitchen door and paused there, glaring at Rudolfi for a moment, then went on through and out of sight.

Bolan told him, "I got those girls back."

Nothing could rob Rudolfi of this supreme moment. He was exultant and almost giddy over his victory, in excellent spirits, and seemingly feeling no ill-will toward anyone, least of all Mack Bolan. He all but fawned over him, in fact, as he replied, "So? Very well. Perhaps this is something we may bargain on, eh?" The cat was teasing the mouse, hugely enjoying the imagined tortures seething through the other mind. "Would you give me back these prostitutes in exchange for your own life?"

Bolan replied, "No, I went through too damn much to get 'em out. Think of something else."

"But no, my friend, it is for *you* to do the thinking. I will give you until the count of five to think of something. Eh?"

Bolan shifted wearily beneath the blanket. "I thought you were going to give me a last drink."

"But of course! Cici! Bring Monsieur Executioner his final refreshment." Rudolfi laughed and advanced closer, savoring each ticking second of this, his greatest moment. "The armies of America did not stop you, as I knew they would not. They are street hoodlums, all guns and guts, no mind and no soul."

"Oh you've got quite a soul," Bolan said weakly. "It takes more than guns and guts to send young girls to Africa. Yeah, you're quite a man, Rudolfi."

The mad eyes blazed in brief anger, then settled back into a happy contemplation of the victim. He was saying, "Think hard, my friend, before—"

Cici came in with the glass of juice, interrupting the gloating taunt.

Bolan told her, "I guess I don't want that. Put it down, then pull off my blanket and get out of here. I want Rudolfi to see my wounds. Wouldn't you like that, Rudolfi?"

The underground ambassador to France was smiling delightedly. "You think I will not shoot a wounded man? What manner of deal is that? What does Rudolfi get from a deal such as this, eh?"

Cici was withdrawing the blanket. Her eyes fell on the machine-pistol in Bolan's hands and in a flash she understood his instructions. She tossed the blanket to the floor and ran lightly toward the door.

Rudolfi was staring at the *pistolet* as though it were a swaying cobra. Bolan was telling him, in that wearied voice, "This baby has a dead-man trigger on it, Rudolfi. One little twitch of my body and it starts talking. At 450 rounds a minute, that means you wouldn't catch probably more than twenty or so slugs in the belly. Or you might get zipped if I twitch too much, just a short incision from the crotch to the throat. That's the only deal I'm offering you, Rudolfi. I'm ready when you are. Go ahead."

Triumph, and exultation, and every sign of living spirit sagged out of the man as he once again contemplated his own death. Bolan had known, and Rudolfi knew that he had known—and this, too, showed in the defeated face, the deadened eyes—the gutless, heartless, soul-less shell of a man who had no right to live and even less reason to die.

The luger wavered, and Rudolfi began moving carefully toward the door, reaching back with the toes and planting them painstakingly in the quiet retreat.

Before he reached the door, Bolan told him, "Next time I see you, Rudolfi, I'll kill you. And the next time I hear of young girls being snatched off to Africa, I'll come here from hell if I have to and I'll rip through this country like nothing you ever imagined."

Without a word Rudolfi backed out of the door and carefully pulled it shut. Bolan left the chair, threw off the lights, and hobbled to the window.

Cici ran over and joined him there. Bolan told her, "He's running down the drive. He won't be back. He just lost his last gut."

"I was sure you would keel heem," Cici said in a choked voice.

"I did," Bolan said tiredly. "The worst way possible."

He tucked the *pistolet* under his arm and headed for the bedroom. "Anyway," he told her, "I couldn't zip him with you standing there looking on. I mean, I figured I owed you that, Cici. You *have* been working for the guy, haven't you?"

She recoiled as though he had struck her across the face. *"Non,"* she murmured, and helped him to the bed, pulled back the covers, and steered him down.

"Well," he sighed, "when you get ready to tell me about it—"

"I am ready now, Mack Bolan." She was whisking off skirt and blouse and preparing to slide in beside him. "I will keep you warm, and 'old you while you sleep, and when you are refresh—well, may-bee Cici will discovaire what you do othaire than sit and look, eh stand-in?"

He was grinning weakly and holding out his good arm for her to slip into, and she was continuing her speech.

"But for Rudolfi, I did not know until this vairy morning of 'is unsavory eenvolvements, you see. But I do know thees man for many years. My seester, you see, Roxanne Loureau, she is 'is confidential secretary, among othaire things. And Roxanne 'as call me, you see—a vairy smart woman, my seester—she is suspect soonaire than anywan 'oo thees Gil Martin really is, you see—but she fears for her Rudolfi, not for Mack Bolan. And so she desires for Cici to get thees dangerous man out of Paris, you see, but she does not tell Cici 'oo this savage man truly is, you see. And when I found out, I know also now 'oo is truly thees terrible Rudolfi, and—"

Bolan said, "Shut up, Cici. And welcome to Eden."

"What means this?" she asked, rising above his face to peer down into his eyes.

He pulled her on down, discovering that maybe he was not all that weary, after all—and gave her a non-verbal mouth-to-mouth translation of his message.

Yeah, yeah. There was an Eden for every man, even for an executioner.

It could not last forever, of course—but for a man who had learned to live for every heartbeat, a short visit in Eden could seem an eternity. For the moment, Mack Bolan was ready to *live* and willing to *love*. And so also, it seemed, was Cici Carceaux.

Bolan should have known better. Through the window came a reminder from hell itself, in a crash of thunder and the sulphur smell of gunpowder and a nine millimeter projectile streaking so close to the flesh as to lightly singe his belly. The thunder rolled on and things were tearing into the mattress and pillows, something warm and wet was oozing across Bolan's torso, and Cici's breath left her in a soft little "Ohhh."

His hand was groping on the floor for the *pistolet* even before his mind realized it and then he was firing from the bed, a blazing X pattern smashing the bedroom window and finding solid impact material just beyond. Something hit the ground out there and threshed about, the firing ceased, and there was mind now only for Cici—Cici, raised to one elbow and dumbly contemplating a flow of blood from her abdomen—Cici, staring at him with the question of life in her eyes.

Rudolfi's terrified voice was weakly shrieking pleas for help from somewhere outside Eden, but Bolan had neither time nor inclination to hear or heed. He made a compress of the sheet and pressed it harshly against Cici's wound, guided her hands to it and showed her how to hold the pressure, then he staggered through a red fog to the telephone and summoned emergency assistance. He gathered his clothes and put them on while Cici—brave little sex darling of Europe who was now paying the bill for Bolan's weakness—watched him with unreproving eyes and pleaded with him to get away from there.

"There weel be anothaire time," she assured him.

He knelt beside the bed and held her until the siren turned into the drive, then he solemnly kissed her goodbye and went out through the rear of the house. Rudolfi lay there on the patio, zipped from right shoulder to left hip, his time fully run out. Bolan stepped over him and went down the steps to the boat landing, started the cruiser, and headed into the Mediterranean.

Behind him lay not life but death, not victory in any real sense but merely a prolongation of an impossible war. Ahead lay new battlefronts, an endless succession of Rudolfis and Lavagnis—this grim truth softened somewhat by the certainty that there would also be more Martins, Browns, Walkers and . . . yes, perhaps even another Carceaux. But no . . . He gave the cruiser full throttle and swept south toward tomorrow's front.

No . . . there would never be another Cici Carceaux. He had come frighteningly close to canceling out the only one around—through his own softness, his own shrinking from an executioner's destiny and that near-fatal reach for Eden. It would not happen again. The only safe enemy was a dead one. A single plan of action lay now in Mack Bolan's future—the creation of safe enemies.

He sighed, lit a cigarette, and turned to gaze back at the rapidly receding shore. He had learned an important truth back there. Yeah. There were no crossovers from hell to paradise.

Goodbye, Eden.

Hello, Hell.

Lookout, Mafia. The Executioner is sweeping on.

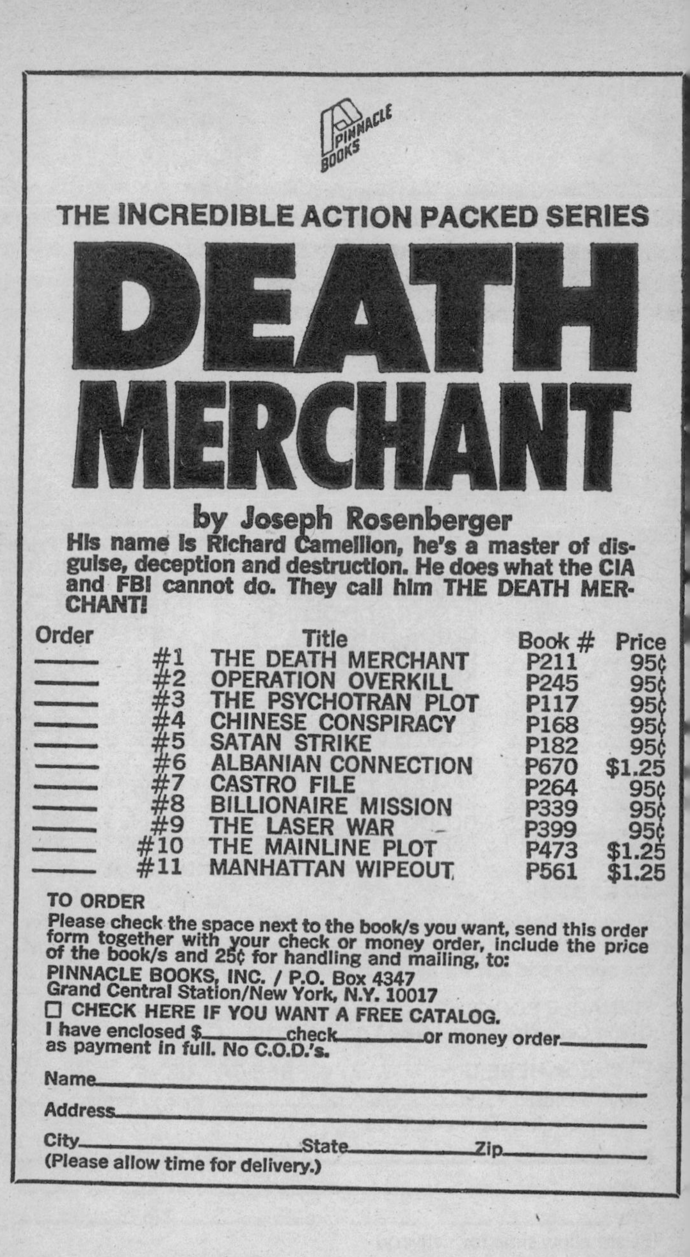